NAOMI

NAOMI

Berniece Rabe

THOMAS NELSON INC., PUBLISHERS
Nashville, Tennessee / New York, New York

Library of Congress Cataloging in Publication Data

Rabe, Berniece.
  Naomi.

  SUMMARY: During the 1930's a Missouri farm girl is told by a fortune-teller that she will die before she is fourteen.
  [1. Farm-life—Missouri—Fiction   2. Family life—Fiction]   I. Title.
PZ7.R105Nao   [Fic]   75–4599
ISBN 0–8407–6444–8

For My Daughter—

DARA RABE

NAOMI

In southeast Missouri in the thirties, when a woman's survival depended on marriage and a man's survival depended on the hard work and frugality of his woman, Mom's task was to teach her daughters, early, the requirements for getting and holding a husband.

Superstition and taboos still played important roles in the lives of these God-fearing people. However, a parent's teaching, trying, wishing, or forcing must bow to Fate, which had the final say in a child's destiny, just as it was Fate that had the first say in the child's physical appearance at birth.

No one asked eleven-year-old Naomi if she wished to be reared with these philosophies. She didn't have a say in the matter at all. Or did she?

—B. R.

ONE

"Cain't y'hear? I asked you what y're doin'?" Grace shouted.

Naomi paid no attention to the roughness in her sister Grace's voice, but kept right on with what she was doing, placing one leg with a great crossing motion in front of the other as she walked on the hard-packed dirt path that circled their weathered house and made forks through the weeds to the barn, chicken house, toilet, and cotton field. "I'm walkin' like a cow. What does it look like I'm doin'?"

"Well, Mom says to cut it out. She said for me to tell you that it looks nasty."

Naomi took two more cow steps.

"Better stop it right now, or she'll wear you out," Grace warned.

Naomi looked down at her feet to make sure she was doing the cow walk just right and kept going. When Mom looked at a cow, her only comment was of milk and cream and churning butter, but Naomi saw more than that. Mom said life was full of necessity and hard work and you didn't need to look farther. "Work's work! Now keep your mind set to it, and if there's time to play, then git out from under foot and do it, but first comes work!"

It didn't take any more time to notice that a cow, with all her crossed steps, still took a straight path, but Naomi didn't let Mom know that she enjoyed such things. Mom hated anything that resembled pretending.

Just the same, nobody, not even Mom, could see inside a person's mind, so Naomi often pretended. It was good company. What with a whole family of boys, who went their own way, and Mom and Grace, who took to each other, things could get lonely for Naomi.

"Naomi! If you ain't goin' to quit it, then git on out behind the chicken house so's Mom don't see you."

Grace stood there solid as an oak, her arms crossed. Dad called Grace his little oak and Naomi his tall willow. He himself looked like the catalpa whose leaves were broad like his hands, face, and shoulders. Naomi had said that to him once, hoping it'd make him take time for a talk. It didn't. He just smiled and went his way. A man's place was in the fields with his sons and not around the house chatting with daughters.

Right now, Mom was forcing Dad to stretch his noon hour so the two of them could talk in private. She had shooed Naomi and Grace outside. Maybe if Naomi listened she'd hear Dad use some more of the picture names he had for people. No, the talk was too low, although a couple of times Mom's voice grew loud and Naomi heard the word "Wilma."

It hadn't been lonely when Aunt Wilma was alive and living with them. Aunt Wilma, Dad's youngest sister, had died two years ago of a water-moccasin bite. She had been pigeon-toed. Naomi changed her cow walk and took a few steps in the bouncy toed-in way of Aunt Wilma. Aunt Wilma couldn't pull a sack of cotton. Abe, Naomi's oldest and favorite brother, said it was because of deformed hips. Naomi figured it was because Aunt Wilma had rather be doing other things, like petting a cat, or making clover chains or a surprise birthday cake, or rolling butter into fancy little balls. At the thought of butter Naomi's steps took on the walk of a cow again.

Mom hated Aunt Wilma, and that was awful. It was a sin to hate the dead.

Aunt Wilma's self portrait, which hung among the bright red roses of the living-room wallpaper, made her look pale and womanly. Her pale-yellow hair, tiny face, and big round brown eyes always had folks noticing and commenting, "I swear, Naomi, you're the spittin' image of your Aunt Wilma." Actually Naomi took her brown eyes after Dad, but no one noticed that, because Dad's face was big and always sunbrowned. He was an outdoor man even in the coldest weather.

Grace had blue eyes like Mom's. The entire family was known as the yellow-haired Bradleys, but that didn't mean they all looked alike. The fact that Naomi and Grace measured out even height didn't mean a thing either. Lots of little things made one person different from another. Naomi knew she was different from any other person in the whole world, dead or alive.

"Naomi!" Grace's voice was as forceful as Mom's. "I'm going in and tell Dad you're bein' spiteful and tryin' to worry Mom."

Naomi kept cow-walking and thinking as it pleased her to do. Mom always worried, regardless. Like most farm women, Mom worried for fear her daughters would never get married and have a home of their own. Naomi had heard it often, because that was the way Mom's worry talk went for daughters. For the boys it was, "Wonder if Pete'll have a weakness for drink, like Cousin Luke? Wonder if Paul will ever put in a full day's work in his life? Wonder if Jay will ever be able to hire out when he cain't git them rows he's plowin' lookin' like somethin' other than a nervous snake!"

13

Being grown up and getting married was a long way off. Even the five hours until suppertime and the chore of bringing in the cows seemed a long way off. Mom didn't need to do all that much worrying, anyway. Naomi could chop the weeds from more rows of cotton in a day than Pete, and once she had used a garden plow and had made rows as straight as the railroad tracks that ran in front of their house. Mom didn't need to worry about her younger daughter becoming a useless old maid. At least Dad never worried about her.

Grace unfolded her arms, coughed a warning, and started toward the back porch. Quickly Naomi stopped her cow walk and matched Grace's heavy strides until they neared the porch steps. Grace looked pleased with her victory but said nothing.

Naomi wondered what the silence was for when Grace raised her finger. "Sh-h," she said.

Naomi hesitated about huddling low beneath the solid bottom of the screen door with Grace. She had made a secret vow to Preacher Haller last Sunday to cut out all her sinful ways, but she first had to decide whether eavesdropping on Mom and Dad's talk was a sin or not. Their voices were rising. She sure didn't want Grace to learn more things than she. Grace was ten months older and that was enough of a head start.

But wasn't Mom always saying, "Naomi, you've got to start listenin' to your elders!"? All right then! Naomi scrunched low on the step next to Grace and listened.

Mom said, "Her second baby, and she ain't married yet! Mr. Walker warned she'd turn out to be that kind of woman, and she has. He named her sort when she weren't more'n eleven years old. There ain't a worse sin in the eyes of the Lord, less'n it be murder. Oh, Lordy, two of 'em!"

Dad said. "It puzzles me how Mr. Walker can call them

right all the time. I pity the Jacksons, even that old swamp-wallow, Curt Jackson. Girls at the least are a burden to a man, but to have one turn out bad . . . well, a body cain't tell how his kids'll turn out! An' you can tell least when it's your own you're puzzlin' over."

Girls were not burdens! Dad couldn't be worrying about her, could he? He never had—or had he, and she just hadn't known? Here she sat, eleven years old, the exact same age Faith Jackson had been when Mr. Walker predicted Faith's outcome.

Keeping low, Naomi inched nearer to Grace and whispered, "Why don't Dad know how we'll turn out? I know how I'm turnin' out! How does Mr. Walker know somethin' that Dad don't when they're both growed men?"

"Sh-h-h. Naomi, you don't know nothin'. Only Fate knows how a person will turn out, and Mr. Walker's got the gift of knowing what Fate's got in store. Ever'one around knows that."

Grace often stuck around Mom and listened when she talked to the visiting neighbors. Naomi didn't bother listening as a rule. It interfered with her own thinking. "I ain't goin' to be like Faith Jackson! Dad's got no right to worry!"

"Well, you're the spittin' image of Aunt Wilma, ain't you? Mom says she was a burden and stayed one all her life!"

"I ain't being a burden. I'm gonna be rich!"

"Be rich, and you'll go to hell!"

"No, I won't! The Bible says a rich *man* cain't go to heaven." She talked as loud as she dared, trying to get some sense through to Grace. "God didn't make that rule for women, only men, or He'd've said so. Mom says it's a sin to add to the Scriptures."

"Sh. There ain't no use shoutin' about it. Anyway, if I was you, I'd be afraid to shout somethin' that was a lie

15

in the first place." Grace slid to the far end of the step and folded her arms.

Naomi would have said more, but Mom was talking again. "Oh, Mr. Walker knowed all right. Poor Mrs. Jackson, she done the best she knowed how by Faith, and the good Lord cain't expect no more'n that, I reckon. Her main fault was in sparin' the rod. If she'd followed what the Good Book says, maybe things would have took a different turn, but some women is weak. What Fate has already set would take a world of beatin' to git out anyway. . . . Oh, lan's, lan's, two of 'em!"

Naomi couldn't bear to hear Mom praise lickings, so she turned her back to the door. "Why's Mom gittin' so mad about Faith's havin' two babies? Mom's had a baby ever' year, if you count the three little girls that died. And now that Uncle Dwayne's twin boys'll be coming for the summer, she'll have nine kids right here. So what's so bad about Faith havin' two babies if she wants two babies?"

"Faith ain't married, that's what makes it a sin," Grace answered. Grace sure enjoyed sounding smart, as if she knew everything.

"What difference does it make whether she buys her babies before or after she's married?"

Grace got that disgusted look on her face again. "Naomi! I'll bet you think that Fluffy went out and bought her kittens!"

It wasn't fair for Grace to be ten months older; she knew all kinds of secret things. Grace spent her whole time eavesdropping—that was how she knew so much. Another ten months and . . . Well, maybe eavesdropping was a sin if you listened too much, or to certain things, like Grace, who even listened in on their older brothers' private talks. But maybe just hearing a few words . . . Dad was talking now, and since Preacher Haller had said

16

time and again, "Naomi, be good and listen to your parents," she listened some more.

Dad was still speaking with awe. "I ain't knowed of a case that Mr. Walker has missed on. He said Sarah Mitchell was losin' her senses before Dr. Foster owned up to the fact that maybe she was a might odd, but that old hickory nut let her go right on bein' a nurse, travelin' the countryside like a man. And remember how Mr. Walker told us all that Jim Haller would end up preachin'? And when he said it, Jim was tearin' the town apart. Mr. Walker ain't called a wrong one yet. It's . . ."

Mom interrupted. "I'd sure like to hear what he's got to say about—" Mom's words stopped the instant Naomi's back bumped against the screen door. Chairs were moving, and in a second the scolding would begin. Naomi leaped from the step and casually began to walk like a cow. By the time Mom's words began, Grace had joined her in the cow walk too.

"You kids! I'll teach you to eavesdrop! Long ears!"

Dad was in the doorway now with Mom, and he was wiping his big hand across his brow as if giving himself time to collect the happenings. "What you girls doin'?"

"We're playin' cow walk."

"Now look here, that's no way for little ladies to walk." Dad didn't look very happy, but he wasn't nearly so angry as Mom. No one could see the color of her eyes now; they were squinted almost shut, and her teeth stayed clamped tight until Dad finished his say. Then she took her turn. Naomi started to whistle closely, softly, a trick she had got hold of. The small sound helped to drown out the words coming from Mom.

"Grace, I sent you out before to tell Naomi to cut that out. I've a good mind to give you a switchin' for lettin' her go and entice you to do the same thing. Naomi, cut out that whistlin'! A whistlin' girl and a crowin' hen always comes to some bad end. Look where that sun is already! Grace, come in the house and help me make dinner. Naomi, you git that bucket of coal oil and bug the potaters. We was jist talkin' about the potaters needin' buggin', wasn't we, Dad? Now go on, or I'll git my switch!"

Grace always got the house chores. "I cain't carry that big bucket of coal oil all the way to the high ground," wailed Naomi. "It'll slosh all over my legs and make a rash." She was angry with Dad and wanted him to know it. "It's wrong to plant potatoes in an Indian graveyard, any-way."

Dad said, "You can cut such talk, Naomi. That was more than likely their campsite, not their graveyard. It's fertile ground—that's why the crop is good. Now run along."

Mom snapped, "The crop's good because I had them potaters set out in the wane of the moon. Well, don't jist stand there, Naomi. Git the funnel and pour some of that coal oil back into the can. That'll stop the sloshin' and stop your excuses."

If Abe were here, Naomi bet he'd know how to win an argument with Mom and get her out of the nasty job of bugging potatoes. She hated potatoes, except for maybe finding an arrowhead at digging time. Oh, she liked their taste, but it wasn't worth the bugging and the peeling of them. Abe had argued with Mom the last time Mom screamed at her about how she peeled them. "Naomi," she had yelled, "you'll never hold a husband with peels that thick!"

Abe, who'd just come in the back door to find the file and had heard every word, spoke right out. "Mom, will you stop yellin' at Naomi about a husband. She's jist eleven years old."

Mom had hit Abe on the ear with the potato she had been examining. "I'll thank you not to tell me what

18

to do! Your dad'll hear about this. He may let you run the cotton field, but *I* run the kitchen. I cain't and won't abide a wasteful woman in my kitchen. I put up with one for eight years until the Lord relieved me of my burden. Naomi's jist like her. You'd think your Aunt Wilma was back from the dead and had peeled that potater herself!"

That didn't end the argument with Abe. "Mom, I'm not talkin' about Aunt Wilma. I jist want you to cut out all this harpin' to Naomi about marriage. She's only eleven, for cat's sakes!"

"Please, Abe, I'm old enough to chop cotton and—"

Mom wouldn't let anyone else join her argument with Abe. "I was married and had you on the way, Abe, when I was fifteen! Four years ain't a long time. Listen to me. *I* know." Mom started to walk away, then added, "That Mabel Russel of yours, she's sixteen, and I got eyes, I give you another three months. Now no sass. Your Dad's sister or not, Wilma had looks enough to've been married at sixteen at least, but she died at twenty-one, still a burden on us. Eating like a horse, for all her dainty ways, and food as scarce as hen's teeth! Well, I thank the Lord for deliverin' me of my burden!"

"Mom, Aunt Wilma was the prettiest and the best woman I ever saw."

"Purty is as purty does! A good woman works hard, gits her own home."

Abe caught Mom's hand as she struck out at him. "Mom, she was crippled. You're not. Naomi, you'd be better off in the field with us, hoein'."

Abe sure knew how to win an argument. The following week he got a job with a rich farmer who lived twenty miles east. Abe got to live in a fine house and earn pay as a hired man.

Getting paid could make most any job easier, even bugging potatoes, Naomi thought. She set the coal-oil bucket down to rest for a moment. The potato patch was halfway between her home and Sarah Mitchell's painted house. A strange woman, that Sarah Mitchell. Mom said nurses who lived alone and ran about the country alone were not women to pattern after, were not really proper women at all. But Sarah grew pretty flowers. Tulips.

In the science book at school it showed that a tulip had a stamen and pistil. Her teacher wanted them to bring a sample of a stamen and pistil to school, but the book showed only a tulip having such and no one had tulips except Sarah Mitchell. Who would dare step in among her pretty flowers? Reela Russel said she'd pay anyone twenty-five cents for one of those tulips to take to the teacher.

Naomi turned away from seeing the tempting flowers and looked back at her own house. The afternoon sun lay easy now on the gray unpainted siding, making it look cool and inviting as it sat high on its two-foot blocks, ready to catch every breeze. Five wild rose bushes made spots of color between the outbuildings, the enclosed horse lot, and the dirt yard with its sparse shoots of grass. Too bad wild roses didn't seem to have stamens and pistils.

If Naomi had a rich father who worked on a railroad like Mr. Russel, she'd pay someone twenty-five cents for a tulip too. But that would be stealing, for they belonged to Sarah Mitchell, as did the canna bed and the hedge that grew near her shiny white house. Pumpkins and watermelons grew in the sandy soil next to Naomi's house. It was as if the corn, clover, and oat fields had come to a stop and then backed off a bit to make room for the house and barn. Too bad clover flowers didn't have a stamen and pistil, or potato blossoms. Naomi picked up the coal-oil bucket and tramped on.

Mom said that she had more than Sarah Mitchell because Fate had blessed her with a hard-working man.

Dad said he'd surely found himself a fine hard-working woman when he found Mom. Naomi liked to watch his eyes when he talked like that about Mom. If only Dad wouldn't be so doubtful when it came to believing in Naomi and how she'd turn out. Did so much really depend on Fate, the way Grace said?

Naomi could be as hard a worker as the next person. She stepped up to a potato vine and knocked a big, fat, juicy orange-and-black potato bug into the bucket of kerosene and watched it die. Bad things had to die, and that took care of one horrible bug. But there were hundreds more on that one plant and jillions more in the rest of the patch.

This was the worst of all kinds of work and, all the while, Grace was getting to help Mom in the house. Always Naomi obeyed Mom, but why should she do this nasty job of bugging potatoes if it so happened that Fate would have her turn out bad like Faith Jackson or, even worse, make her an everlasting old maid like Aunt Wilma just because she couldn't peel a thin potato peel? It wasn't worth it. Even Dad wasn't sure how she'd turn out!

Naomi plopped down the kerosene bucket. If she did work hard it wasn't going to be for nothing. If she was destined to turn out bad anyway, then why mind Mom? Maybe she had bugged her last potato. She would just go into town and ask Mr. Walker how she was going to turn out. If he said "Good," then she would come back and tolerate bugging potatoes.

Yes, she could walk to Malden now, ask her question, and be back within an hour. That way, she could still get some bugging done before quitting time. No one knew just how long it took to bug potatoes, so . . .

The main street in town was still outlined with bits and scraps of trash from the weekend. Wrappers from Popsicles blown next to the store fronts, and empty tobacco sacks lay scattered under each half-log resting bench along the way. The men that lined the benches every Saturday were gone, but the neck of a brown whiskey bottle stuck out from the grass. Naomi picked it up and smelled it. *Yech!* So that was the odor of the stuff that could ruin a good man!

She hurried on past Mr. Bell's grocery store and the movie house. Then her steps slowed and halted. She was getting near Mr. Walker's shoe-repair shop. A huge man's shoe, made of wood, with the top and heel almost rotted away, hung over the front door. On the big glass window in scratched red paint a sign read, *John Walker's Shoe Repair. Come to me, I'll save your sole.*

No use hesitating about what had to be done. Naomi opened the door of the repair shop. A little bell jingled. She closed the door and opened it again in order to hear the bell ring a second time. The smell of the shop was sharp, a bit like the smell of the harnesses that hung in the barn and the axle grease that Dad used on the wagon. No one was there. She touched a tall boot and then reached for a very wide belt that had been sewn three times on the diagonal. Wonder how a fat belt like that got broken. Wonder why folks decided that sewing could be man's work if it was on shoes and belts, but woman's work if it was on dresses or cotton sacks.

Suddenly Naomi was aware of Mr. Walker standing too close. Her hand jerked away from the wide belt. Unlike Dad, Mr. Walker was a short man, made up of little hills. His cheeks were rosy hills, his stomach a smooth sloping hill, and his buttocks stuck out separately in back in two equally round hills. He began talking friendly before she had time to say her polite "Hi."

"Well . . . you must be one of the Bradley girls. You got the black eyes and the Bradley yeller hair. That's

22

a fine combination." He wiped his bulgy round fingers on his black apron. "You'll be a looker one of these days."

"Will I?"

"Yup, a right smart looker. Who fixed them shoes for you, little lady?"

"Oh, these?" Naomi looked at her high black shoes. "Dad, he fixes all our shoes," she explained. "He's got a shoe last in ever' size. He couldn't nail the sole back on 'cause there was nothin' to nail it to. That's why he wired it on. I'd rather go barefoot, but there's copperheads in the potater patch, and that kind of snake don't give no warnin'."

"Now hold on a minute here." Mr. Walker reached toward her shoe. "Did you come to git me to glue that sole on?"

"No."

"You havin' trouble with the snakes in the potato patch?"

"No."

"Then you better sit down and tell me your business." Mr. Walker motioned toward a long wooden bench. His words ended quickly now without tapering. Was he impatient?

"I don't need to sit. I jist wont you to tell me how I'm goin' to turn out." Naomi heard the sound of her own heartbeat and wondered if Mr. Walker could hear it too.

"Now hold on just a minute, little lady. Just set down like I told you and spell this all out."

"I jist need to know, that's all." Naomi moved away to an old cane-backed chair across from Mr. Walker.

"Y'got troubles? Somebody been botherin' you?"

"My mom and dad's been botherin' me—about how I'm goin' to turn out when I'm grown up. I hope Fate don't make me turn out bad, 'cause then I'd have to turn Catholic like Aunt Wilma so's I wouldn't go to hell. Catholics have a place in between. I don't want to turn Catholic. Mom says that if—"

"Look, honey, I ain't no preacher. Y'might discuss that

particular question with Brother Haller." He stopped his words short again and kept looking at her, waiting. It made her uneasy. Why didn't he just answer her questions?

"Did you do somethin' to rile your dad and mom?"

"No, sir." She clicked the wire on her shoe against the metal sewing-machine stand, keeping her eyes on her feet and away from the piercing eyes of Mr. Walker. "I got to git back. Jist tell me how I'm goin' to turn out."

Mr. Walker crossed his arms over his smooth sloping stomach. "I got two questions. Do y'obey your parents, and have they taught you what's expected in a lady?"

That took some thinking to answer. She did obey much more than Grace. That was a fact. She answered, "Yes. I obey." The fact that she was in town now was not disobeying. No one had warned her against going. There was no actual rule against it.

Now . . . had she learned what it takes to be a lady? She knew that a lady did not walk like a cow, did not hang out around ditches swimming naked like boys, did not get babies before she was married. And she peeled a thin peeling on a potato. "Yes, sir, I know what it takes to be a lady."

She sure hoped Mom had not looked toward the potato patch. She'd been gone long enough. She wished Mr. Walker would take his hand off his chin and tell her what she'd come to find out.

"Well, I'll tell you, little miss, a beautiful woman and a good woman ain't hardly ever one in the same, but you got a fair chance of bein' both."

Hurray! She was going to be a decent woman! And Dad said Mr. Walker had never called a one wrong yet!

"Thank you, I'm obliged to you. I gotta git back to buggin' potaters. G'bye!" She ran out the door, heard the pretty jingle, and quickly reached back and closed it again to hear the bell twice. Then she started the mile run back home.

Now if she only knew whether she was going to be rich

or not. Mr. Walker never told anything except about good-
ness or badness. It took a fortune-teller to tell a thing like
being rich. Fortune-tellers cost money. Dad always said it
took money to make money. Mrs. Jeno, the fortune-teller
who had come to Malden two months ago, charged twenty-
five cents. Now how could she ever earn twenty-five cents?
She'd have to pray about that.

TWO

The Lord provided a way! Naomi didn't know why she hadn't noticed it before but one lone tulip grew on the right-of-way in front of Sarah Mitchell's house. It wasn't even near the velvety green lawn grass that covered every inch of the yard except for the flower beds. It wasn't within four feet of the perfect row of tulips that lined the path to the door. Since it was quite near the road and not actually on Sarah Mitchell's property, it belonged to the public, and she had as much right as the next person to take it. Reela Russel said she'd pay twenty-five cents for one of Sarah Mitchell's tulips, and twenty-five cents was all it took to pay Mrs. Jeno to tell Naomi that she would indeed be a rich woman one day.

As Naomi bent to break off the beautiful red-and-black flower, a voice called, "What . . . no . . . stop it!"

Sarah Mitchell came running across her grassy yard and stopped right beside Naomi. "Who gave you permission to pull my flower?"

Naomi didn't answer. She couldn't answer. Sarah Mitchell looked pretty and neat in a long brown housecoat, which was soft and silky to match her hair, but her eyes were furious. The tulip stuck to Naomi's hand. It was so pretty. She had never touched one before. She stood very still.

"None of you have the right to pull my flowers. None of you, even you, little girl. Who are you?"

"Naomi Bradley." What else was she supposed to say? "I'm eleven years old and the spittin' image of my Aunt Wilma, who is dead." That still didn't seem to be enough, because Sarah Mitchell stood silently waiting. Naomi held the tulip with the sweaty stem out toward her. "You can have it. I just wanted to take it to school. We're studying flowers."

"Take it, Naomi Bradley," said Sarah Mitchell. "But don't touch my flowers again. All right?"

"All right, Sarah Mitchell."

Naomi started to leave, but Sarah Mitchell stood there, tall and slim, as if wanting to say more. Finally she said, "There must be flowers. One mustn't destroy the flowers. I couldn't bring myself to uproot that stray one. The blossom just opened today, you know." Sarah Mitchell turned sadly away, and Naomi ran with the flower toward school.

Reela Russel said she'd get the money the next day. She said it was worth the twenty-five cents to be the only girl in eighth grade to bring a flower, the only one in school to bring a tulip.

Once Naomi had the twenty-five cents, all she needed was to think of a way to trick Grace into going along with her to see this strange Mrs. Jeno. She couldn't tell Grace why she was going because Grace would tattle to Mom that Naomi wanted to be a rich woman. Dad mustn't know either, for he said there never was and never would be anyone who could tell fortunes. Mom said fortune-tellers were of the devil.

Grace believed in fortune-tellers. She said old Grandma Harney, who lived with her husband over on Seven Ditch, had given Mrs. Jeno twenty-five cents of her pension money to find their missing yellow cat. Grace said the cat came back the very next day after being gone eight weeks! Grace said she believed that Mrs. Jeno was a real fortune-teller, even if

Curt Jackson did say she couldn't hold a light to the one way over at Poplar Bluff. Mr. Jackson claimed Mrs. Jeno was a phony and couldn't tell fortunes any more than a ground hog. Mr. Jackson, such a skinny little man with his round fat belly, was always talking too much. People should say that *he* was bad instead of his daughter Faith and her two babies.

Naomi carried the money with her, waiting for the right day, the right time. For sure one day Grace would start some talk and everything would happen just right, and Grace would end up wanting to do the very thing Naomi needed her to do.

It took a few weeks, but Naomi used the time to get used to the idea of facing a real fortune-teller. The day it happened Naomi was sitting near the road ditch, jangling the coins in her dress pocket, and letting her dreams form while she braided some dandelion stems. It would be great to be rich. She'd give gifts to everyone who needed anything. She'd smile as she saw Dad fussing and fuming, embarrassed something furious when he had to own up to the fact that his daughter Naomi was not now nor ever would be a burden.

"What y'doin' with that money?"

Grace stood above her. Naomi tried to remember whether she had been thinking out loud. "What money? What y'talkin' about?"

"Y'got from Reela Russel. I saw her give you something awhile back. I'd been wondering. So it *was* money. Did you git her out of some kind of trouble, is that why she paid you money? What're you goin' to buy? How much you got?" Oh, Grace was curious!

Curiosity! That was the thing that would get Grace to go along with her to the mysterious little house where Mrs. Jeno had come to live and raise her five children. Dad said there wasn't a thing mysterious about the little shack old man Jeno had left to his dead son's widow and kids. Just the same, Naomi would feel better if Grace came along with her. If she worked on Grace's curiosity enough, she'd have her begging to come along.

It was true that Grace never let go of a thing that she wanted to know. Even Mom had warned Grace that curiosity kills the cat, but no warning stopped her. When Grace got curious, people might as well give in and give up. That was fine.

"If I tell you, d'y' promise to cross your heart and hope to die if y'tell anyone anythang about it?"

Grace crossed her heart and hoped to die.

"Well, I thought . . . You know how grown-ups go to see Mrs. Jeno, the fortune-teller? I'm going to be the first kid in the whole country to see her!"

Grace's face was wild with surprise, and her voice came in a pleading whisper, "Take me with you. Take me with you, Naomi, or I'll tell Mom. I swear I'll tell Mom!"

"You jist crossed your heart that y'wouldn't, so you cain't."

She said that to make Grace angry. Let Grace beg some more so she'd think it was her own way she was getting.

Grace pleaded and threatened and begged and suffered before Naomi gave in. She couldn't stand to see anyone suffer that long.

After a bit, she said, "Grace, how are we goin' to find a time to see Mrs. Jeno without Dad and Mom findin' out?"

Grace was so relieved by the question that she had an answer coming out immediately: "The twins are comin' to-morrer, and Mom won't leave 'em, so it'll be me and you ridin' into town with Dad to git groceries. Mom never leaves the twins with us the first day they come."

Grace was absolutely right. Mom loved to help out the sick and dying and the poor and needy—at least the first day. She felt the Lord was adding stars to her crown in heaven when she took care of her brother's motherless twins. Naomi knew from years before that as soon as Mom had her good feeling and started noticing the extra work with the twins, she would give Naomi the job of minding them.

Anyway . . . when the twins did arrive on Saturday, right off Mom said, "Well, this means I cain't go into town to buy my groceries. The least I can do for my brother's little motherless kids is stay home with 'em and get 'em settled in. Pore little tykes. The Good Book says take care of widders and orphans. Look at 'em. They don't get fed right in town."

Benny and Bruce were not settling in, they were running like wild in every direction at once, or least it seemed that way, with both of them dressed alike in cut-off overalls and tennis shoes. Twins were something to watch! Every boy in the family, Ike, Jay, Pete, and Paul, as well as Dad, had come to watch them chase their legs off.

Dad said, "Let 'em run. The rest of you kids, come pile in the pickup and leave Mom handle them little boll weevils in her own way."

Ike and Jay sat up front with Dad, and Paul and Pete sat on the tailgate. Naomi hunched up out of the way of the wind with Grace beside her behind the cab.

Grace whispered, "See, I was right, wasn't I? I said it'd be jist that way, didn't I?"

Grace needn't act so self-satisfied. "Grace, jist 'cause you're ten months older don't make me have to listen."

Naomi continued sitting next to her sister anyway. It was sort of nice having Grace do something interesting with her for a change. Usually Mom kept the two of them apart on all work jobs, with Grace staying near Mom, and Naomi set at work by herself with her thoughts. It was nice doing something and being able to talk about it with a listener. She talked to Grace all the way into town.

The minute the truck came to a stop in front of the grocery store, their brothers were out and running toward the baseball diamond on the school ground. Naomi asked Dad, "You need me and Grace? Or can we go look in the winder of the dime store?" She was afraid Dad would expect them to help do choosing like Mom.

Dad smiled. "Run along and try to stay outa meanness. Your Mom has ever'thang all wrote out, and I'm warnin' both you girls right now not to make any fuss, 'cause she wrote on here to git a couple a candy sticks for the twins. Now she's bribin' them rascals to be good, and you girls are too big for bribin'. You be good or I'll tan your hide. Now run."

As they walked toward the door, Naomi heard Mr. Bell say, "Them girls is sure sproutin' tall."

Dad answered, "Yep, that Naomi is growin' like a willow, and she's jist about caught up with Grace. Give her a couple more years and . . ."

The door closed out Dad's voice, and Naomi headed toward the dime store.

Grace yelled, "Mrs. Jeno lives this other way! Where y'goin'?"

"I asked Dad if we could look in the dime store, and I cain't go back on my word."

In the dime-store window was a huge jar brimful of penny candy. She could buy twenty-five pieces with the money in her pocket. The thought was almost too much to bear. But God didn't give her this money for something so frivolous as candy. He gave it to her to set her mind at ease. Knowing that she would turn out a fine lady had certainly made life easier, and knowing for sure that she'd be rich could make a lot of things take on a difference. She could buy the whole jar when she got rich. She'd spend the money on what God aimed it for.

Naomi ran to catch Grace. "Grace, when we get there, I'll let you do the knockin'."

"If I knock, she'll thank it's me wontin' to see her. Are

y'gettin' worried that Mrs. Jeno might tell y'somethin' y'don't wont to hear?"

"She ain't goin to tell me somethin' bad. Fortune-tellers don't tell bad things!"

"Some do. I've heard of some that do. That one at the carnival two years ago, he told Mr. Jackson to watch out for fallin' timber, and right after that he got his ankle broke when he and Mrs. Jackson was clearin' ground."

Naomi couldn't be bothered even answering Grace. All Grace ever knew was what she heard. Naomi had actually been to *see* Mr. Walker, and he had given her the nicest answer. Mrs. Jeno would probably say, "You're goin' to be the richest woman in these parts and never a burden to no one. It's your absolute Fate to be a rich woman!"

Even if she said the worst thing in the world, like, "Your Fate is set also in the spittin' image of your Aunt Wilma. You'll be an old maid and a big burden . . ." well, even if Mrs. Jeno said that, Naomi wouldn't care. She'd just be glad to know it. She'd do what she pleased starting the minute she got home. She'd pretend she was sick and stay home from church and cook in Mom's kitchen. The next Sunday she'd go swimming in the ditch while they were all at church, and the next Sunday she'd ride old Turner or Jill. There'd be no use in trying to please God or Dad or Mom if you knew it was a losing battle. It didn't matter what Mrs. Jeno said, she'd be ready. Nonetheless a cool chill swept over Naomi's body, making her shake.

Grace stopped to look at the goose pimples on Naomi's arms. "What's the matter? Why are you shakin'? Are you gettin' scared, Naomi?"

"O' course not. I'll do my own knockin'!"

On and on they went for four blocks until they came to a little faded yellow house set way back from the road and nearly hidden by hundreds of giant hollyhocks. The hollyhocks were pretty, some dark pink, others light pink, and still others in shades of purple. They made walking closer a bit easier.

Naomi thought she would go right up to the door and act just as if she were going to visit her best friend Mary Jean Kruse. She'd knock loud enough to be heard. As she neared the door, she raised her hand to knock. At the same time she started to close her eyes to help the pretending a little. Suddenly, before her knuckles touched the wood, the door flew open. That proved right off that Mrs. Jeno was a real fortune-teller.

"You girls come to see me?"

Grace didn't make a move or say anything or act curious or anything. She just stood there staring. No one could blame her, because Mrs. Jeno didn't look like a fortune-teller. She looked just like any other town woman, with pale skin and the darkest eyes in the world. They were lots darker than the Bradley eyes, which were considered the darkest in the county. She didn't have any scarf wrapped around her head either, and she wasn't wearing one thing of velvet.

Mrs. Jeno stepped back from the door for a second to yell. "You kids, get on out back like I told you!"

She yelled at her children like any other mother. The only thing different from common was that she was beautiful. Mom had never spoken of a pretty fortune-teller, and Grandma Harney hadn't said a word about her being pretty. Even though her long mass of black hair was stringy and her dress was ripped at the side seams, she was beautiful.

Mrs. Jeno started tapping her foot. Naomi hadn't meant to stare. Staring is a mean thing to do. She'd have to start talking.

"I got twenty-five cents. That's the right money, ain't it?"

Mrs. Jeno pushed the hair up from her forehead and smiled a right nice smile as she held the rusty screen open just a bit wider. "Come on in. What in the world is botherin' you two?"

34

She motioned toward a divan whose back rest was made of a dirty brown corduroy and whose cushions were of a greenish-gray mohair. No store ever sold a divan like that, it had to be nothing but a makeshift. Grace sat on it. Naomi stood. How was it that a fortune-teller could be poor too? Why didn't she just go find a hidden treasure? That would make sense. But maybe fortune-tellers couldn't tell things for themselves. Dr. Foster had to go to St. Louis to get himself doctored.

Naomi meant to ask her question real quick and then leave. "Mrs. Jeno, I hear y'can tell if a body is goin' to be rich and stuff like that. I jist want to know if I'm goin' to be rich?"

Grace squealed, "Is that what you wanted to know, Naomi? Well for—"

"Good gosh, you kids ain't no different than the grown-ups. I was afraid you had a serious problem."

Naomi didn't like the laughter in Mrs. Jeno's voice. Being a burden was a serious problem. Mom talked about it all the time, and it was awful the way Mom still acted hurt toward Aunt Wilma, even though she had been dead for two years, so it must be a serious problem to be a burden on relatives.

Mrs. Jeno was a small woman, but her arms had strength as she pulled Naomi down into a chair near where she herself chose to sit. A little table made of woven baling wire with a piece of window glass for the top stood between their chairs. On it lay a deck of cards. Mrs. Jeno picked up the cards and started spreading them around. She was mumbling something. Then she went to a dresser and got more cards and added them to the first bunch and mumbled some more.

At last she sat back and looked up toward the ceiling for a long time. Her eyes weren't actually shut, but a body could tell she wasn't seeing out of them. There was magic in this room! Mrs. Jeno *was* a real fortune-teller.

Naomi thought the silence would never end. It was quieter than when they buried Aunt Wilma. Mrs. Jeno finally looked back at the cards, pushed the little table aside, and said with a soft but determined voice, "I cain't take your money, honey." Then she added roughly, "You kids run along! Run along."

Mrs. Jeno knew something. You could tell it by the feel in the room and the look on her face. Even Grace felt it and was no longer staring. "What is Naomi's fortune?" she demanded. "You got to tell her!"

"You got to tell me, Mrs. Jeno. I gotta know. Oh, I gotta know!"

Mrs. Jeno sealed her lips solid for a second and then again said roughly, "There ain't any fortune. Now run along."

Grace was on her feet at once. "Yes, there is, I know there is. Everyone that pays their money gets a fortune told, and you gotta give Naomi hers!"

Mrs. Jeno was beginning to look angry now and snapped at Grace, "Look, kid, all I gotta do is scrounge up food or die. Go!"

Naomi thought it was a good idea to leave, and she started to, but Grace seemed her old self now. Bold as ever, she blurted out, "You ain't no real fortune-teller! Mr. Jackson said so. And now the whole town's goin' to know it for sure! You cain't make no livin' in this town, for Mr. Jackson says—"

At the sound of Mr. Jackson's name, Mrs. Jeno's face changed, first to a greater anger, then into a slow smile. Again her expression seemed full of concern as she looked directly at Naomi. "Look, I don't wanta do this. It ain't worth the twenty-five cents." She looked down at the cards again and kept her glance low as she said, "Honey, you ain't never gonna be rich. You ain't gonna live to see your fourteenth birthday. Make the most of your years. Don't waste them. *Promise* me that! It's the only reason I'm tellin' you. I'd as soon die myself as have to tell you, but . . . well, life can be hard, harder than dyin'."

No more! Naomi could listen to no more. Words were still coming from Mrs. Jeno's lips, but Naomi could not understand any of them. Her eyes began to burn, and her head pounded like a thousand hammers. She couldn't think, didn't want to think.

She found herself walking toward the door. Grace caught up to her and jerked her to a stop. "Give her the twenty-five cents. She told your fortune and y're keepin' the money."

Naomi reached into her pocket and handed Mrs. Jeno the twenty-five cents.

"No, no, I told you it's not worth it to me." But Mrs. Jeno's words seemed to hang in the air with no meaning. Anyway, she took the money, then looked at it in her hand and said, "Heaven knows, my kids have got to eat, too."

Naomi was opening the screen door and Grace was pushing against her when Mrs. Jeno added, "You can tell Mr. Jackson that he'll see the day when he'll listen to my words! He'll know I got the gift, that I cain't make things up."

Naomi wasn't concerned with Mr. Jackson. Mrs. Jeno's words were starting to hit now, and she fought against the tears so she could see her way to follow Grace back to the pickup. She needed to go home.

Her brothers didn't notice how terrible she felt. They were too busy with their own noisy talk and laughter. Pete begged them all to ride in the truck bed so they could sing. Grace, with a look of horror on her face, sat at the other end of the truck bed far away from Naomi as if she were already a corpse.

Naomi also wanted to be far away from Grace. She needed to think. She jumped out and went up front to ride in the cab with Dad, but she didn't dare discuss such things with him. He'd say Mrs. Jeno wasn't a real fortune-teller, just a mean woman! But Naomi remembered those dark, sad eyes when the words came out about death. . . .

Oh, shucks, thinking didn't help a bit. She was going to meet her Maker! Now she heard Preacher Haller's sermons coming back sharp and clear, full of meaning. Oh, she did believe in Heaven and Hell. She just hadn't planned to give it any serious thought until she was as old as Grandma and Grandpa Harney.

Jay once said there wasn't any sense in taking life too seriously. And Paul had said that a person ought to enjoy life because you lived only once. Right after Paul said that, Preacher Haller gave a loud sermon on the subject. "Some of you believe y'll jist eat, drink, and be merry, for tomorrer y'may die, that you ought to live it up in this one life y'got. But, brothers, death is only the beginnin' of a second life. I've yet to see a man who didn't believe in a future, who didn't go wild and wreck his life right here and now. Hear my warnin'! What we are in the next life is determined by what we are in this one. Ever' last one of us will have to pay for ever' act we do—for even the thoughts we thank!"

What awful thoughts she'd had! She'd even planned on missing church. No, she hadn't actually planned to do that, for she hadn't really expected Mrs. Jeno to say that she'd be a burden. Well, Mrs. Jeno hadn't said *that*. What right did Mrs. Jeno have to warn her about death? She hadn't asked about death.

But once your Fate had been told and you had been warned, there was just no way to change the matter. No way at all. Once there was a story in a newspaper about a girl drowning in a horse trough on the very date a fortune-teller had said she would die by drowning. That girl had stayed away from ditches and rivers from the day she got her warning, but it still happened just as prophesied.

Naomi curled herself tight in the corner of the front seat

and tried to think of other things. It didn't help, though, for she thought only of the nightmares she had had after going to the graveyard with Dad and standing there and watching him fill in the sunken grave of Aunt Wilma. Death meant the end to everything unless you believed in Jesus and went to Heaven, or were Catholic like Aunt Wilma and got stuck at that place in between. Mom said that Catholics were of the devil and were all going to Hell, but that couldn't be so because Aunt Wilma was good, and she was Catholic.

Naomi didn't want to die. She didn't want to go to Hell. No one was perfect except Jesus. How could anyone be sure where they would go? Preacher Haller said little children were young and innocent and God overlooked some of their meanness. How old did a person have to be before God expected them to be perfect? She moved a little closer to Dad, wishing to talk, but when she saw him sitting so contentedly, whistling a bobwhite tune, she moved back to the corner again.

She waited a few more minutes until she just had to ask, "Dad, is it set whether a person is good or bad by the time they turn fourteen?" Her voice trembled, but she couldn't help it.

Dad seemed to notice now that she was troubled. "Naomi, you come up with some strange ones! I never could figure out where you git all your questions from. I'd expect it's pretty set, but then, on the other hand, maybe it ain't. Cain't always tell. Some folks have a wild streak, then settle down later on in life. Most likely it's set for girls, but not some boys."

"Well, what if a body died at fourteen and it wasn't settled yet? Would God put them in Heaven or Hell? Things was settled with Aunt Wilma, weren't they?"

"Naomi! Stop them fool questions and git your mind workin' on somethin' useful. Recite your times tables."

She obeyed Dad. But it seemed just like that movie show Abe took her to once where they were going to shoot a man and all the firing men had to count to ten first. Only instead of counting, she was saying "Six times nine equals fifty-four, seven times nine equals sixty-three."

She started saying her tables out loud and that helped some. Soon her lips were saying "Five times nine is forty-five," but her brain was remembering Dad one night declaring loud and forceful to all the whole supper table, "Cut out such talk! There ain't no such thing as ghosts nor fortune-tellers nor any sort of magic!" At the time, Naomi hadn't believed him, for she was little and scared of the dark, but now she wanted to believe him. She wished she could talk to Dad. He was so big and strong, and she needed to talk to him. Couldn't he see that?

Back home everyone had to help carry in the supplies. Mom made all but the twins run along outside so she could give the little boys their treat, and no one would have to suffer watching them eat it.

Naomi headed for the chicken house, but when Grace tried to follow, she went on out past the woodpile instead. Grace joined her anyway.

"Go away!"

"Gee, Naomi, I didn't know she was gonna say that! I cross my heart and hope to—"

"Go away. I'm not gonna die! I'm not gonna die!"

"Yes, you are, Naomi. If Mrs. Jeno said you was gonna die, then you will. She knows ahead of time when a body's number is up. She's a fortune-teller, and you ain't!"

"Who's a fortune-teller?" A voice boomed out behind them.

There stood Mom pulling down the baling wire that had been strung across the chicken-house door to keep out that old brown hound dog that had been coming around sucking eggs. "What's this about a fortune-teller? Now own up! Grace, you better tell me, and right now!"

Even before Grace did it, Naomi knew that she would tattle, because Grace, generally speaking, stayed on the good side of Mom and hardly ever got a licking.

Grace said, "Mrs. Jeno told Naomi she's gonna die 'fore she's fourteen! Ain't it awful?"

Mom turned to Naomi. "Did you pay that woman? I hear she charges twenty-five cents. Where could you git that kind of— Did you pay her?"

Naomi nodded. You couldn't do anything else when Mom asked a question. She was so mighty, so powerful, and she was really mad. When Mom got mad, no one had better cross her or she'd hit with whatever was handy.

"Where'd you git the money?" Naomi didn't plan to answer, but it made no difference. The wire came slashing down across her legs as Mom pulled her forward. Once, twice, three, four times, the wire bit into her bare legs and across her arms as she struggled against the pain. Above her screams came Mom's shrill voice yelling, "Payin' good money to a servant of the devil! I'll never have it said that I put my sanction on such acts. Don't ever let me hear of you goin' to that woman again!"

Dad came running and yelling now, and the boys ran up too. Mom stopped beating to explain to Dad. "This girl's paid twenty-five cents to hear she's goin' to die! She paid that devil Jeno good hard money to hear that!" Naomi clutched at her bleeding legs as Mom went on talking. "No, I won't allow it! I'll not spare no rod."

"Better stick to using a switch! Control yourself at least long enough to get a switch. Naomi, you go take care of them legs, and you forgit what that pokeberry told you! Pokeberries look pretty, but swaller them, and you're poisoned!"

"Daddy, Daddy, I cain't forgit it. I jist cain't. I tried!"

"Well, I'm tellin' you to forgit it! There ain't no such thing as a body being able to tell the future. She gits her wash rained on same as the next one. She cain't tell nobody's fortune, least of all when a body'll die. Forgit it! Hear? Now don't y'ever let me hear you mention it again!" Dad walked away.

The boys all stood around, looking. Bruce and Benny, the twins, were crying so loud that no one's words made sense until Jay scooped them onto his shoulders to silence them.

Pete said, "That's right, forgit it, Naomi. She ain't no more a fortune-teller than I am. She was out tellin' a bunch of people last week that we'd live to see the day, not too terrible far off, when our sky would be buzzin' with airplanes, and, heck, we're lucky if we see one pass over these parts once a year."

"Yeah," said Paul, "and when one does, it's so unusual the whole school gits to run out and look. Yeah, best you forgit it, Naomi. A nut, that's what she is."

Ike said, "He's right. We worry enough about things we already know. Ain't no use addin' to it."

Everyone, except Mom, who had finished rolling up the baling wire and had gone into the house, was still standing there looking solemn. Finally Pete added, "Naomi, I tell you, Mrs. Jeno *is* nuts! You want to hear somethin' else funny? She said that Mrs. Jackson was going to get skinny as a rail and die. Now, that's about as farfetched as you could get. Mrs. Jackson is strong as two men and fat as a hog and healthy as can be."

Nobody said any more, and Naomi limped over to the pump to wash her wounds. Everyone else found another direction to take.

That's just what she'd do, she'd forget it. No one was going to make her die before she reached fourteen. No one! She'd try very, very hard to forget it.

42

THREE

Naomi couldn't forget. When she tried to put Mrs. Jeno's words out of her mind, she just naturally got to thinking more and more about dying and ended up remembering all the stronger the thing she was trying to forget.

Dad had an answer to the problem right off. "Work. Git your mind on somethin' else!"

But she had chopped cotton from sunup to sundown, and it had kept her so busy that sometimes, when no one was looking, she sat down to rest. Still, her brain kept right on thinking about Mrs. Jeno's words.

When Paul caught her crying and found out why, he said, "Remember how Pete kept bettin' me I'd strike out at baseball practice? His harpin' made me mad, but I still struck out. Then I got to thinkin' how I could benefit by such harpin'. I went to Jay and got him to bet that I'd make a homer—and I did!"

Naomi didn't see just how Paul's baseball story fit in with her worrying about having to die, unless he was trying to tell her to go to another fortune-teller, maybe the one over at Poplar Bluff, and get him to say that she wouldn't die, after all—sort of like the Good Fairy in *Sleeping*

Beauty. But fortune-tellers didn't place bets or set spells, they just told what Fate had in store.

It did cheer her up a bit when Dad bragged about her for chopping more cotton than either Pete or Paul. Dad said that she was so good that when she grew up he was going to let her hire out for pay, even if she was a girl! She could see herself getting rich for being the fastest girl in the world with a hoe, but then Mrs. Jeno's words came galloping back in to wreck the vision.

She had to forget those words! She was going to live, and she was going to be rich too. Wait and see! Grace said that no woman ever got rich unless she married a rich man, but some people said that Sarah Mitchell had lots of money, and she wasn't married at all, so Grace didn't know everything!

Naomi immediately hunted Grace up and told her, "Grace, you don't know ever'thang."

"I do too. What is it I don't know? Naomi, you better tell me."

"I can chop more cotton than the boys, so that proves I ain't a burden. Right?"

Grace just glared at Naomi for a while, then she shouted, "You still rememberin' that? You're stupid. Girls ain't burdens unless they live in the same house with their brother like Aunt Wilma did."

"I ain't gonna be no burden. I'm not like Aunt Wilma."

Grace plainly didn't care and didn't want to talk about it. She started to walk away but stopped to say, "I guess you won't be no burden if you're dead."

"I ain't gonna die! Grace, I told you before, I don't aim to die."

"If your number is up, you'll die. Ever'body has to die when their number's up. Mrs. Jeno jist told you when yours is up."

"She oughtn' to've told me. It's wrong! God won't let it happen, because it's wrong for Mrs. Jeno to tell."

Grace didn't seem bothered by that explanation. "Sure, he'll let it happen; he's the one to set the number in the first place. Mrs. Jeno claims she did right in tellin' you so you'd not waste your life away."

Naomi spit at Grace, and Grace went running to tell Mom. Let her run, let her tattle. She hated Grace for saying her days were numbered, and she hated Grace for being right again. Preacher Haller warned people repeatedly to search the Scriptures so they might set their lives in order for the time when their hour comes. Her own hour was coming too soon. She should be searching the Scriptures. But she'd tried once, and all that "Judah begat Pharez" and such stuff didn't make sense. When Preacher Haller talked, it made sense, but he was away, holding a revival meeting at Parma. Just who did she have left to talk to? She'd already tried Dad and Paul and Grace. Mom, of course, was not to be considered.

Right when things looked blackest and Naomi's memory of Mrs. Jeno's words was the sharpest, Grace came running in with the news that Abe had some days off and was coming home for a short visit.

Of all the people in the world, Abe was the one who really cared for her. He would listen to her worries, and he'd have answers, the right answers, and he'd spend a long time discussing them with her. Abe, whose full name was Abraham, was as good as the man in the Bible for whom he was named. Mom chose that name for her first boy. Then came Isaac, which got shortened to Ike, and after that, Jay, short for Jacob, and then Pete, for Peter. Last came Paul, who said no one would shorten his name or he'd be damned. God overlooked swearing in boys.

After Mom had lost three girl babies at their birth, she had prayed for another to live and be a help to her around the house, and by the grace of God, she got Grace. Mom promised God that if he'd give her yet another girl, she

45

would name her Naomi. But just before Naomi was born, Aunt Wilma had come to live with the family and it had put a mark on Mom, causing Naomi to be born looking the very image of Aunt Wilma.

Mom never went back on her promise to the Lord about the name. Naomi was the last child and Abe the first, but they were the dearest of friends. Abe was tall and handsome and very strong and had always loved her. Abe could take on any one of the other brothers. When he wrestled, it was something to see. Strength poured out of every muscle, and his face and scalp boiled red under his blond hair and eyebrows. Yet, with all his power, Naomi could show him a woolly worm, and he would stop to caress it.

The very minute he got home, even before he got through saying "Hi" to everyone, he bent down to Naomi and whispered, "Naomi, want to see somethin' real pretty?" And he placed in her hands a tiny pair of slippers all covered with powder-white fur and with no backs on them at all.

"Oh, Abe, they're beautiful! But they're way too little for me! Anyway, they're made funny." She sat down on the floor so that her skirt spread out to cover her big feet.

Dad said she had big feet because it was natural for a tall girl to have big feet, but they seemed entirely too big for the rest of her. Mom had said, "Naomi, y'better keep your feet covered! It'll be hard for you to catch a beau with them feet o' yourn!" Naomi had decided to smile a lot and take people's eyes away from her feet.

Abe's chuckling made her look back at him. "They're not for you, Naomi. They're for my girl. They'll fit."

They *would* fit Mabel Russel. Mrs. Russel and all her daughters, Mabel, Reela, and Dolly, were lovely, and with the exception of Reela, they were all small. Naomi imagined Abe carrying little Mabel across the threshold when they got married, but Mom always said no upright, respectable farm woman would allow herself to be toted around like a baby.

Naomi held the baby-soft little shoe in the palm of her hand, and Abe said, "You think they look funny? They're not regular shoes. They're called mules."

She laughed, and all the boys, standing around waiting for Abe to stop talking with her, began to roar with laughter.

"Speakin' of mules," Paul said, "come out to the barn. I want to show you the gash where old Turner got hung up on the singletree the last time we had a runaway."

Abe looked away from Naomi and gave his attention to Paul. "Okay, and wait until I tell you about where we can get us some beautiful horses. Dirt cheap, too. Jist a minute here, let me give Naomi somethin'. You like pretty things? You can have this locket here. Darn thang turned green, and I couldn't give it to Mabel. It's yourn if you want it." He handed her a little heart-shaped locket that shone yellow gold where it wasn't tarnished. Then he went to the barn with the boys.

It was all right. Abe had given her a gift, hadn't he? He did have to spend some time with the boys at the barn. She'd let him get his horse talk done. She liked to listen to it, too, but girls neither went out to the barn with the men, nor were supposed to like horses. Naomi liked horses a lot, but she could wait. She'd go out alone during the day, as usual. Right now she'd best shine her locket. She took it and jabbed it back and forth in the loose dirt under the edge of the house, scouring it as clean as she did the table knives before company. Tomorrow morning she'd talk to Abe, after he'd had a good night's rest.

The next morning she dressed hurriedly and ran upstairs. Her younger brothers slept in one room and her older brothers slept in the big beds in the room with the sloping ceiling nearest the stairs. Abe was still in bed, and she woke him playfully. He had his eyes half shut, but a big smile crossed his face, and his arms reached out to catch her. She felt wonderfully happy when he held her with one big muscular arm and grabbed a feather pillow and pushed it into her face with the other.

But the play lasted for only a moment. Abe sat up and said, "Hey, run along now, so's I can git dressed. I promised the boys I'd hike into town with them, since the ground's too wet to be in the fields. They're down eatin' already."

"Can I go too? I want to go with you." She knew she couldn't stop his plans, but she could at least join in with them.

"Naw, you don't want to go runnin' around with a bunch of boys. It's no place for a girl. You stay home and help Mom make that big dinner she promised me today. You wouldn't have any fun with us at all."

"Yes, I would. I promise. I'll have more fun than any-body!" She grabbed his arm. "I need to talk to you, Abe. Please, let me go!"

Abe patted her gently on the shoulder, but said with final-ity, "No, honey, this is strictly for boys."

He couldn't mean it! She waited for Abe to change his words, but it was like waiting for a schoolteacher to notice your hand when you had the right answer. Instead, it was Paul who answered. There he stood at the head of the stairs with his glass of milk still in his hand. "We're goin' out lookin' at motorcycles. We don't want no girls taggin' along! You stay in the house where y'belong and help Grace take care of the twins." Paul finished gulping his milk and started back down the stairs. "Come on, Abe. Ever'one's ready but you. Grab a glass of milk and let's go."

Instantly Abe was dressed and on his way. Naomi sat on the stairs and listened as the screen door slammed behind them.

If she were only four years old like the twins, she

wouldn't mind being left behind. She was eleven and then some, plenty old enough to talk and laugh and look at things with her brothers. She hadn't planned to talk about Mrs. Jeno the whole time, just for a few minutes when she had a chance to be alone with Abe. Abe would've settled things fast and then she could've gone right on back to laughing and having fun like the rest.

It was because she was a girl that they wouldn't let her go. They never let Grace go either, but Grace hadn't begged to go. Grace didn't even want to go because Mom was going to let her make biscuits today. If Grace did want to go, she'd just sneak off and do it. That's exactly what Grace would do.

Naomi jumped from the stair and dashed out the back door. She ran as fast as she could across the backyard before Mom got a chance to see her.

Oh, no, Spot was loping right behind her. "You cain't go, Spot. This is no place for dogs. You'd just git in the way."

It took some doing to make Spot stay home where he belonged. Finally, she was able to sneak on out into the corn patch and take a shortcut through the rows over to the railroad track. She hid in the bushes along the railroad right-of-way and waited. Pretty soon she heard her happy brothers making their way down the track. They were laughing so loud that she had to shout to be heard.

"Slowpokes! It'll be noon before we git into town."

Boy, were they surprised! Pete and Paul both acted as if they'd seen a ghost. The laughing had stopped.

Naomi balanced herself on the rail and walked several feet closer to them. Anyone who could walk that far on a rail without teetering was worthy to be taken along.

But no one paid her a compliment. Instead, Ike grabbed her by the collar, lifted her off the rails, turned her around, and pointed her toward home. "All right, now let's see jist how far y'can walk them rails back in the other direction." It was terrible. Everyone, even Abe, was telling her to get on back home where she belonged. How could Abe be like that when she needed him? Maybe his voice was a little more gentle, but he was saying the same thing as the rest. He didn't care either. If he had cared, the least he could have done was hit Ike.

Naomi refused to walk one step toward home, but stood and glared at them so they could see just how mean she felt. She felt as mean as an old copperhead ready to bite at the first chance.

The boys began laughing again and turned toward town, leaving her to stand alone. They knew she wouldn't follow. Sure, they knew it, because they were big and had strong muscles and they were five, and she was only one. She kicked a cinder toward them, and deep groans came from her throat. Because she had no other choice, she started walking the tracks back toward home. When she was dead, they'd be sorry!

The sun was hot now, and it made the berries growing near the edge of the track look bright red. She reached out to pick some of the extra large ones. The berries slipped from her hand as an instinctive alertness swept through her body. A snake slid away near her foot where it had been sunning. It wasn't a copperhead, or even a water moccasin like the one that had killed Aunt Wilma, but just a garter snake. Paul said that garter snakes were perfectly harmless, and the only reason he ever killed one was because they scared the girls. Well, she wasn't scared, and Paul wasn't so smart! She could be as brave as any boy.

Jay sometimes took garter snakes by the tail and whipped off their heads. He'd won a lot of money on bets doing it. She would do that. She would prove that girls could be as brave and as strong as boys!

Naomi's arms were rigid with fright, but she forced her hands out to grab the snake by the tail. She had it! She had the worst of all creatures in her hands.

50

Naomi couldn't help screaming wildly as she thrashed the snake about, hitting it again and again against the rails until it was quite dead. It took so long. It was as if she'd never actually known before that a snake had muscles filled with strength and force that battled for life just like—well just like . . .

She ran ahead a few feet and began dry vomiting until her stomach tightened into a painful knot. She couldn't think about it. She wouldn't think about it. She hadn't taken the life of a human. God Himself had put a curse on serpents. It wasn't the same as other life. . . . She would not think of it! She'd count to a hundred by nine's . . . three times . . . backwards. Why had she done it? Oh, dear, oh, gee, his number was up—that was why she'd done it. Oh, dear. Nine, eighteen, thirty-six . . .

She walked with her head low looking at the dirt path that angled across the right-of-way and led toward home. Often she took this path to come sit and wait for a train to go by.

Naomi decided to wait for the train. One was due pretty soon, and it was good to be doing a familiar pleasant thing. The trainmen liked her. They always waved and threw her a newspaper.

She sat down in the middle of the path. Why did boys hate girls so? There never had been an answer to that question. Maybe her brothers were jealous. At least Paul was, for he showed it. Recently, when Dad bought the groceries, he'd managed to tuck in a little bag of gumdrops or coconut bonbons in a corner of the grocery box. Mom would empty the bag into her aproned lap as soon as he got home and divide the candy among *all* the children equally.

But division doesn't always come out even, so any leftovers went to the twins and the girls. Paul said it was damned unfair to give more to girls just because they were girls, but Naomi couldn't help what Mom did. She hated Paul. She hated all her brothers—and Grace too. She couldn't talk to Mom, and she couldn't talk to Dad. She wished she were—

The train whistled, and she jumped up to wave at the fireman and engineer. She hoped the "paper" man was in the caboose today. Yep, there he was. She waved vigorously at him too, and the man threw down a rolled-up copy of the *Kansas City Star* and shouted, as usual, "Give it to your dad!" She was glad to get a paper today. At least it would please Dad. Mom never read the paper.

But Dad wasn't home, and Mom, who was busy sweeping, didn't look up from her work. Her forehead was beaded with sweat, but her dirty working apron covered a clean, starched print dress. Naomi noticed that her own job of clearing the breakfast dishes was already done. The dirty dishes were stacked neatly at the end of the long table, waiting for her to wash them.

It would be best not to mention that she was hungry from having skipped breakfast. She slid quietly past Mom and went straight to the food-storage safe to get a cold biscuit and make herself a sugar sandwich.

"Don't mess up that floor! You'll have to wait to wash them dishes till the floor's all dry! You been hidin' out agin? You been out readin' books when there's work to be done? It'll catch up with you one of these days, and watch out when it does! And watch what you're doin' with that sugar! I don't want ants swarmin' in here all year round."

Naomi broke open a second biscuit, spread it with butter and sugar too, then went outside to eat and drop crumbs in peace.

The twins, Bruce and Benny, both wearing striped trainman overalls, came running up, calling in their high-pitched voices, "Come preach us a funeral, Naomi! Please, Grace won't do it."

"I'm eatin' right now," she answered.

"But we're all ready! Benny made a wreath, and I fixed

the casket. Come on. It's time for the preachin'." Bruce's big blue eyes pleaded as he tugged at her hand. Those twins!

His touch sent a warm feeling of love through her, and she gulped her last bite and put her arms around the little boys. Who could resist these two cotton tops? Jesus loved little children, and he wanted everyone else to love them too.

Naomi hated to admit it, even to herself, but she'd once been jealous of all the attention Mom gave the twins. Her friend Mary Jean Kruse had explained that it was the same in her family, that grown-ups felt easy making over little kids. Now Naomi really understood. It was easy to like and be liked by small children. These little boys didn't turn you away or kick you when you wanted to be with them or talk to them. Why, they were the ones who were doing the begging! They really wanted to be with her! She took each little boy by the hand. It'd be good for her to play with them. It'd help get her mind off her own problems.

"Sure, I'll preach you a funeral," she said. "Who you buryin'?"

FOUR

Bruce said, "Grace hates woolly worms. She won't preach no funeral for somethin' she hates."

Naomi knew why Grace wouldn't preach the funeral. Mom had spanked both of them once for preaching a funeral for a big red ant. Mom said the Lord doesn't magnify himself through a woman and that funerals were sacred and weren't for playacting. Grace said that was why she never preached any more funerals, but likely the real reason was because Grace never listened close in church to Preacher Haller and never knew the right words to say. Grace usually found a way to do things she really wanted to do.

Naomi checked to see if Mom was around. She was in the garden, so it was safe to do the funeral for the twins' benefit. When you were feeling low, it helped to do something you were especially good at and to do it for someone who appreciated you. She told the twins, "I'll be with you in a minute. Let me git myself in a preachin' mood first."

She stopped at the pump house with its mossy roof and woven-wire sides full of climbing honeysuckle. Little ruby-throated hummingbirds darted in and out. She poured a can of priming water into the rusty pump and then pumped herself a drink. She slapped water in her face and around her neck. It felt nice and cool and gave her time to think up a sermon. The smell of the sweet honeysuckle was right for a funeral mood. She practiced lowering her voice to a sad tone, then followed the twins around to the front porch.

The ground under a house that sits on wood pilings always stays dry and is easy to dig. She noticed that the grave was already dug there. In fact, the twins had not done badly with the whole setup. Maybe the dandelion wreath was a little too large for the yellow-and-brown woolly worm, but it required at least five blooms to make a circle, and Benny had used just that number. As she started to pick up the glass casket, which was really the broken-off neck of a vinegar jug, Bruce cautioned her to watch out for the jagged edges. What made him think to use the neck of a vinegar jug to make a casket? He was very smart for his age. She was proud to be his cousin.

She stood on the porch and started to preach. "All right, set down in the front row on the ground there." She leaned forward and whispered, "What's his name?"

"He ain't got no name."

"Well, y'better think of one fast. I cain't preach a funeral with no name."

"His name is Fuzzy," Bruce whispered.

"Dearly Beloved, we are gathered here to pay our last respects to our friend Fuzzy, whose number was up. It's mighty nice to see you all here today. There ain't no doubt in my mind that Fuzzy here is goin' to Heaven. He was a worm that was both good and handsome. He never did like the idea of goin' to Hell. He knew the laws and rules and where his place was, and did what all a worm is supposed to do. He never wasted his life but crawled the straight and narrow. I'm sure he'd have been as good at flyin' too if he'd had the chance to be a butterfly." She paused, because even with bowed head, she saw Grace slip in and sit behind the twins. Then she finished with "Let me say in closing, don't do as I do, but do as I say! God rest his soul. Amen." Fuzzy looked peaceful and pretty in his glass casket, lying there quietly in his woolly coat. Her heart went out to him.

Benny handed her some twine and said, "Here's the rope."

She crawled under the porch until she reached the grave. Dust billowed up to halt her breathing a bit as she reached out to place the pieces of twine across the open hole and to hold them down with rocks at each end. She laid the glass casket on top of the twine and gently started to lower it into the grave. "You women and children, turn your backs now. The time for coverin' has come." She pushed dirt into the hole with a couple of swoops of her hand and packed it down with her elbow. Her foot would have done a better job, but she was too cramped up under the porch. "Y'can lay the flowers on now."

Naomi crawled out from under the porch to allow the twins to crawl under, put the wreath on the grave, and wiggle back out.

Grace said, "Mighty fine preachin'! You did as good as Preacher Haller did when they buried Aunt Wilma! Here, here's a chicken for your pay," and she handed Naomi a root.

Suddenly Mom was there too. No one heard her come. Mom slapped the root from Grace's hand. "Cut that out!" Then Mom whacked Naomi a good solid blow between the shoulder blades. "I'll learn y'to cut such shenanigans! Making a mockery of the Lord's words! It says plain and clear in the Bible that a woman keeps her place in church."

"I didn't know . . ."

"You did know!" Mom's eyes were wild.

"But I really didn't. I heard a woman preachin' on the radio."

"Radio! There ought to be a law against some of them stations being broadcast on the air! That woman is the servant of the devil! Naomi, you better watch who y're patternin' your ways after! You'll be meetin' your Maker all too soon!" Mom stopped. She looked as if those last words had slipped out accidentally. "Now come on, both you girls, and help me catch some pullets for dinner."

Naomi had to obey, so she followed Mom to the backyard to catch the chickens. Mom oughtn't to have said what she did. Mom must believe in Mrs. Jeno, too, even if Mrs. Jeno was of the devil.

Naomi wasn't patterning her ways after that radio woman, really. It was Preacher Haller she wanted to be like. Could there be anyone better? He was a fine tall man like Abe. And he was a good man, like Abe used to be before he started chasing his little sister away. Preacher Haller was a little older than Abe. His black, wavy hair drooped lovingly across his forehead and glistened when he got to preaching hard and started sweating. Little drops would drip from the hair strands and disappear onto his suit. God had to be pleased that Naomi was trying to be like Preacher Haller, even if Mom wasn't. It only stood to reason.

Naomi helped Grace start chasing down some young chickens. They'd have caught them a lot faster if Bruce and Benny hadn't started helping and scaring the chickens back in another direction just as the catch was almost a sure thing.

Grace got her chicken first and immediately wrung its neck. As soon as Naomi had a sputtering, fighting chicken in her arms, she took it to Mom.

"Well, wring its neck and git another one! Time's a wastin', and if there's one thing I cain't abide, it's half-done chicken."

Naomi had never wrung a chicken's neck before, and she didn't want to feel it struggle like that snake. She handed it to Grace. Grace grabbed it, wrung its neck with a quick jerk-jerk, and then sent it sailing near the woodpile to continue flopping and falling until it lay entirely dead. Naomi wondered if a chicken had a spirit inside it just like people. If it did, when did the spirit leave? On the first jerk or when it lay completely still? These chickens were young ones. Some got killed young and some were left until they were old. It happened like that with all animals—and people too.

"Land's sake! You'll never make a wife if y'cain't wring a chicken's neck! I try to do the best I can by you but—laws!"

Naomi didn't let Mom's words bother her. Hadn't she killed a snake? That took lots more nerve than killing a chicken. Mom had a lard bucket filled with steaming, scalding water and was waiting impatiently. Naomi caught a second chicken but gave that to Grace too. Mom shook her head, and didn't say a word.

Soon the air was filled with the smell of hot, wet feathers. It was a company smell. They never had chicken except when the chickens first got big enough to kill or when they had company. She plucked away at the wet, sticky feathers. "Mom, what you killin' chickens today for? Is someone comin'?"

"Your brother Abe come home, didn't he?" Mom hadn't quarreled with Abe at all since he'd returned. She was awfully nice, even considerate at times, but Abe wasn't company.

Naomi said, "He ain't—"

She was interrupted by Grace shouting, "Mom, Mom! Come see what the twins have done!"

She and Mom quickly laid down the chickens they were plucking and followed Grace to the cozy brooder house with its great metal cone that spread like a hen's wing to warm the baby chicks. There stood both little boys, big-eyed and waiting. Five baby chickens with their necks wrung lay at their feet.

Immediately Mom paddled both of them. She was beside herself with fury. "The waste! The waste! Oh, the eggs and fresh meat these chickens would have growed to give us. Don't neither of y'ever let me catch you in this brooder house agin!"

The twins looked shocked and hurt by Mom's screaming.

Naomi said, "Mom, they just did what we did."

"You boys leave the chicken killin' to us women. Don't you never lay another hand on my chickens!"

Well, that settled that. She'd never tell Mom about killing the snake when she couldn't do her job as a girl and kill a chicken.

Mom regained control of herself and went on plucking feathers. The twins joined hands and started walking slowly back to the house. Nobody felt like talking. But Naomi could hear talking and laughter too. The older boys were returning! Now Abe would listen to her, and after she got him to listen, she'd ask him her serious question.

She and Grace raced toward them to see who would be the first to tell on the twins. Grace slipped and fell right into the mud hole where Mom had poured out the scalding water. Served her right. Grace had thought she'd be first and hadn't taken the time to run around it.

Grace yelled, "Mom, Mom. Naomi pushed me."

Mom called, "Naomi, git back here this minute!"

Naomi stopped and started back, but couldn't resist a try at explaining. "That's a lie! I did *not* push her."

Mom didn't listen. "Git back here! Git them dishes clean so's we can eat a decent meal!" she ordered.

Anyway, dinner was good. It was just like having company. Dad took the news about the twins with the baby chicks in good spirits, and the older boys even laughed about it. She could tell the twins enjoyed the attention they got. No one, not even Abe, noticed Naomi. They went on enjoying their fried chicken. Dad told his usual company joke about always getting the neck of the chicken. She never had understood why Dad said that, for it was Mom who always ate the chicken necks and the straw-bonnet-shaped back ribs, just like Mrs. Brown and Mrs. Jackson and all other farm women.

Abe said, just as polite as company, "Nothin' tastes better than Mom's chicken and gravy!" She guessed leaving home and then coming back made a great difference in how one got treated.

After dinner the boys all followed Dad out to the front yard to rest in the shade. Naomi quickly finished the dishes and ran to join them. Dad was saying, "We could all stand to hear some of the details about them wild horses, Abe."

Abe was eager to talk, "There's no reason, Dad, that you couldn't have some of the finest horses. I'll keep my eyes open and get some choice ones. None of them horses has sold for more than fifteen dollars a head. They round them up out west where they run wild and send a boxcar load back to my boss. He's let other farmers have some, and I know he'd let me buy one if I wanted it. What do you say?"

All the boys started to talk at once. Paul said, "I'll raise me fifteen dollars if I have to go without a coat." Pete agreed. Ike and Jay started begging Dad to raise the money somehow and get a real riding horse.

Dad said, "Well now, I don't know. Maybe."

Everyone cheered. Naomi got caught up in the excitement herself and started yelling, "I want one too, Abe. Get me a shiny black one like Black Beauty." But nobody seemed to hear her.

Abe said, "Now hold on a minute! They're not exactly riding-horse quality. They've run wild all their life, and they have to be broke to the plow. But I sure saw one last time, a nice high-spirited one, that I'd like to've had the money to buy. One of these days . . . But then, some of them are worse than mules to get to pull a plow. I saw one last week balk worse than any mule."

Paul said, "Oh, no, you didn't! Not worse than Mr. Jackson's mule Trigger. Boy, you should have seen it! Roy Rogers would've dropped dead if he'd 've seen that stubborn mule named after his horse. There was Mr. Jackson standin' and hollerin' his head off, and that Trigger actually leanin' backward and saying as loud with hee-haws, as if he was talkin', that he didn't aim to move a inch."

Everybody, including Abe, was leaning toward Paul, listening. Naomi tried hard to think up a good story so that everyone could listen to her next and so that Abe could see that she was there too.

Paul went on, "Then you know what Mr. Jackson did? He went and got some dog push and put it on Trigger's tail, and when that mule moved, he took the plow and ever'thang with him ninety miles an hour!"

Naomi moved closer to Abe and asked into his ear, "What's dog push?"

"Stuff that stings like turpentine that they smear on the mule to put a little spirit in him. Boy, let me tell you, it does the job too!" Abe explained.

"I killed a snake today," she told them.

"How's regular farm wages in around Sikeston?" Dad asked Abe.

"It sure was a mean ugly one," Naomi said.

"Jist 'bout the same's they pay here," Abe said.

"Do you know—"

She started to say more, but Dad interrupted with "Naomi, cain't y' let a body talk? We're not interested in your pretendin'. Now git in the house where you belong!"

She got up and walked around to the backyard. She had not been pretending, and she never told lies! They didn't believe she could do brave and daring things. She could! They listened to Paul's mule story, but she could tell good stories too. She most definitely could!

Big, gangly Spot came up to Naomi and rubbed against her side. She used to ride the gentle old bird dog like a horse. If Spot had a little more spirit in him, he'd be just as exciting as Abe's wild horses, and then she could tell everyone about how wild and exciting he was.

Then she let the wildness of a strange idea swirl her into action. She grabbed the turpentine bottle off the porch rail and just as fast poured a drop on old Spot's tail.

"Ou-u-u!" His howl was so loud that Dad and the boys came running.

Dad's big hands bit into her arms like a sausage grinder taking fresh pork. Spot, her great old friend, was spinning in circles and yelping like he had never done before in his life. "What have y'done, Naomi?" "What's happenin' to Spot?" "Has Spot gone mad?" Everybody was yelling questions.

She felt the pressure on her arms let up as Dad grabbed the bottle of turpentine from her hands and boomed, "What in the thunderation are y'doin' with this turpentine? Y'tryin' to kill that dog?" Everybody but Spot got quiet for a minute to hear what Dad was saying.

Naomi dashed for an open space and kept running to the end of the lane. Meanwhile, Mom had run out into the side yard and was yelling, "Naomi, git back here! I'll learn you to cut shines! Stop right this minute, y'hear? Y've reached the limit!"

Grace was outside too, shaking her fist and screaming. Even the twins were yelling that Naomi had killed their dog.

Naomi had to run away from the sound of the voices. What had she done to Spot? Abe said stuff like turpentine put spirit into an animal. She hadn't meant to kill him. She could still hear screams and more screams behind her. *Kill! Kill! Kill!* She kept hearing the word.

She guessed everyone in the family had joined in the yelling, but she kept on running. No one followed. She ran like the rabbits that Spot loved to chase, ran until she ached. Then she paused, gulped in more air, and ran on. "Please, God," she prayed, "don't let Spot's number be up!"

She ran on past the potato patch, on and on, until she came to Sarah Mitchell's place. Right in the middle of the big yard was the round canna bed with plants four feet tall and in full bloom. Sarah Mitchell might kill her if she hid among the cannas, but Naomi didn't care. She couldn't run one step more, and nothing worse could happen to her than knowing what she had done to Spot. She wiggled carefully to the center of the canna bed and crouched down the best she could. She swatted a mosquito and looked for a place to wipe the blood. Not on these perfect, strange flowers, planted in such precise order. Sarah Mitchell was an odd woman, but she had order around her and Naomi felt the comfort of that order.

Naomi sat in that crouched position for hours, until her legs ached. The sun set in a great orange glow and was soon replaced by a bright moon and millions of shining stars whose warm glow made the big flowers take on an enchantment.

How could there be such beauty in light of what she had done to Spot? If Spot died, she hoped she would die too, like Mrs. Jeno had said, and if she didn't die, then she'd never, ever allow herself to have any more fun in life. Before, it had seemed awfully important to get Abe to talk to her, to help her find a way to forget Mrs. Jeno's words, but it wasn't worth all this sadness. If Spot's number was up, she'd get all her courage together and ask Sarah Mitchell for some of these beautiful flowers to make a wreath for his

64

grave. Spot was her only real friend in the world, and she had killed him. If he was still alive, he'd have come looking for her. He cared.

A noise. Someone was coming up the gravel path. Was it Sarah Mitchell? Was she really a crazy woman, like Mom said? Naomi sat holding her breath in the middle of Sarah Mitchell's precious flowers. She started to breathe again when she saw it was Abe.

"Come out of there, Naomi," Abe commanded softly.

She stood up. "I cain't go back. How did y'know I was here?"

"A big girl like you cain't sit in a neat bed of flowers without bendin' a few. Now come on with you." Abe's face was calm, with eyes crinkling into teasing patterns.

She wiggled gingerly out so as not to break any canna stems. "I ain't goin' back. Mom and Dad will kill me, and I deserve it! Is Spot dead? Is his number up?"

" 'Course not, silly. Turpentine stops stingin' in a few minutes. Spot's number's not up. Don't you know that he's been such a good old dog that God jist had to add on to his number? He'll be with us a long time yet." He patted her shoulder.

Abe had done it! He'd answered her question! Not only was Spot alive for sure, but Abe had just told her that God adds to your number if you're good! Why, she'd be so good that God would add on to her number until she'd live to be a hundred! Just wait and watch! Wouldn't Mrs. Jeno be surprised! She felt so relieved.

Abe kept talking. "An' I gave Mom and Dad the word. I promise they won't do nothin' to you. I ain't been around for nothin'." Abe sounded sure. Did Mom really listen to him now?

"Abe, I didn't mean to hurt Spot. I was doin' like you said, just tryin' to put spirit in him."

Abe put a big comforting arm around her shoulder, and they started toward home. It was nice walking along in the night with Abe. The rose gold of the kerosene lights from home glowed in the silence.

"I really did kill a snake today. I wasn't lyin'. God knows, I don't lie."

"Naomi, what makes you think y'gotta kill snakes?"

"I thought y'd be proud of me, even if I am a girl, and then y'd talk to me."

Abe stopped and cupped her chin in his big hands. "Listen, little sister, I'm proud of you because y'are a girl. You're the sweetest sister I got. You're a lot like Aunt Wilma. I hope y' grow up happy like her. Now don't go tryin' to kill any more snakes nor go hurtin' any more innocent animals. Stop tryin' to be a boy! I got brothers enough as it is." He rubbed a gentle hand up and down on her arm as he held her close with his big arm about her shoulders again.

"Abe, I promise I won't ever kill anythin' again. I didn't like doin' it."

As they walked on she could hear reassuring barks from Spot in the distance. Everything was fine now. She liked the slight coolness of the night, and she deeply loved Abe. A warm, sweet protected feeling filled her.

"You're right, Abe, I'm goin' to be real good, and you'll always be proud of me." She felt his hand squeeze her arm a little tighter.

She knew what she would do to become so good that God would have to extend her number. She had made up her mind not to worry anymore about Mrs. Jeno's words. She'd found a way to change Fate at last. She would become a preacher like Preacher Haller.

About the best thing that anyone could do was preach. Even if it did make Mom yelling mad, Naomi was still going to preach, for that was her talent. The twins thought so, and even Grace thought so. She'd just forget Mrs. Jeno's words and remember Abe's. "If you're good, God has to add to your number." Abe was a fine brother and a strong man. Why, he could take on ten women the size of Mrs. Jeno!

FIVE

Being good—why, that was no problem at all! It sure was no problem if you compared it with being scared of dying. All it took to be real good was to attend church, sit on the front row, and listen closely to every word Preacher Haller was saying. She listened not only so she could learn to do right and live, but also so she could learn the art of preaching.

Grace said that no one would come to hear a woman preacher, but people would come if the preaching was good enough, and Naomi would be good, real good. Like Preacher Haller, she would preach with might and force to let everyone know that it was Jesus who could save them from sin. She would learn all the right expressions of a good preacher and use them. It was important to look sad and weary when you told all about people in Bible times who sinned something awful and about people here and now who were no better. Preacher Haller never made a move on Sunday that Naomi missed.

But Sunday did not last long enough for her to perfect the art. She practiced during the week, too. When she was taking the cows to pasture, she told old Bossy to lay down

her yoke, give the Lord her burden, and mend her ways—
and not to go over the fence ever again to find sweet
clover that would founder her. She went to the barn and
admonished old Jill to stop setting back on her rump like
humans but to stand up right on all four legs in a proper
manner for a mule. She told Carmel cat to stay clear of Mom
and not to get underfoot, for the Lord couldn't be responsi-
ble for men or animals that went where they didn't belong.

She didn't preach to Spot, because he was such a good
old dog, and the Lord knew it. The Lord came to save the
sinner. No use to preach to perfectly good people, or animals.

By pretending the hayrack out behind the barn was a
preacher's platform, she could preach to a whole church
house packed full of dirty rotten sinners, each one in need
of getting his soul cleansed. By the time she became a real
preacher her voice would ring out with such force that the
whole town of Malden or the whole state of Missouri would
be able to hear her word and profit by it.

Pleased be the Lord! He would bless and smile on Naomi
and give her many more years to her life, increasing her joy
a thousandfold. Great-Aunt Philly had lived to be a hundred and two, and folks said she had been as good as love
itself in her younger days.

Naomi gloried in being righteous and listened politely in
church. She didn't give a whit that Grace, who wasn't
worried about dying and had no special reason to try to
be good, was restless and noisy. Grace played kick-your-
shin with Bruce and Benny, making them act up too. Naomi
closed her ears to their racket and listened to every word of
the sermon.

One Sunday Preacher Haller caught her hand as they
were leaving church and said, "Wait a minute, I gotta
talk to you, Naomi."

Why did he do that? She hadn't been making the noise,

it was Grace. She didn't like Mom and Grace's knowing glances as they politely walked on toward the pickup to allow Preacher Haller time to scold her.

Instead, Preacher Haller stuck out his big hand. A soft, wide smile beamed all over his face, and his eyes crinkled with friendliness, not scolding. "Naomi, I 'preciate your bein' my best listener. But I'd jist like to know the secret of my success. You tell me exactly what it is that I'm doin' so good, and I'll practice a little harder in usin' that particular talent. Why *are* y'gittin' so carried away with my preachin', Naomi?"

His words caught her off guard. " 'Cause I'm plannin' on bein' a preacher myself." She hadn't wanted to tell anyone this secret intent, but she felt good having those words blurt right out in the open. It didn't bother her any that Preacher Haller knew.

He had seriousness in his voice when he asked, "Why y' so set on preachin'?"

She wasn't about to tell him how Mrs. Jeno's words had her scared to death of dying. Only last week Preacher Haller had preached a sermon on how death was a time to rejoice, because we'd all be going back to God. No one should dread death. He'd made that sermon up for Grandma and Grandpa Harney. You could tell he had by the way he looked lovingly and tenderly at them when he ended with "O death, where is thy sting?" He was a tender man, but she didn't want to admit to him, that she herself feared death. Besides, it was bad luck to talk about something sad unless you needed help and just had to. She didn't need help anymore. Abe had answered her question.

Naomi looked into the searching eyes of Preacher Haller and gave him a fairly reasonable answer, "I want to be real good and serve the Lord and help out in His vineyard like y' been tellin' us to."

"Well now, y' don't have to take up preachin' to do that.

There's lots of places in church where we could use a girl. I got a job right now where you could be a mighty big help, and I couldn't thank of a nicer girl to take the part. I'm in dire need of an angel in a little play I've worked up for next Sunday. Y' wouldn't even have to act, jist be yourself."

She gave him an extra-hard handshake. Preacher Haller was a man of God and had same as said that she was an angel. It was the next thing to having God's approval. That ought to add to her number.

But she'd almost forgotten about Mom. Mom had come right close to criticizing Preacher Haller, even if he was a preacher, the last time he had put on a skit in church. Mom had said he was *adding to* the Scriptures. Therefore, Naomi had to say no to Preacher Haller without letting him know any hurtful facts.

"I couldn't," she told him. "I ain't got no costume and Mom don't believe in makin' costumes." That was a truth, so it was all right to say it.

"Look, honey, it ain't the clothes that counts. It's what's inside, here. And with that little smile of yourn and them big brown eyes, you don't need a costume."

"Yes, I do. I'd have to have a costume to be an angel." By now she was seeing herself in flowing robes with a halo like the ones in the Bible storybook at church. If only Mom would let her do it, but she would throw a fit at the first asking.

Preacher Haller mussed Naomi's hair and said, "Yup, I can see that y'gotta have a costume, and I know jist the woman to ask. Mrs. Russel needs to give a hand of help. Do her good to put a little of her efforts out for the Lord."

"Will you do the askin' to Mom?" In spite of Mom's behind-the-back griping she wasn't likely to say no to a preacher face to face.

"I will. I sure will," promised Preacher Haller.

72

Of course he kept his promise. Mom was sullen, but later that day, when he arrived carrying a beautiful white dress, she politely let him come in.

Naomi ran forward and touched the soft material. "It's the purtiest dress in the whole world! I don't git to keep it, do I?" The flowers that trimmed the neck and skirt were surely made of pure gold thread!

Preacher Haller hung his head as if hating to answer. "Well, no, Naomi. It's jist a loan. Reela's way too big for that dress, but Mrs. Russel still considers it's hers. She's pretty tore up about Reela goin' off to the city to live with that new husband of hers and, well . . . you enjoy wearin' it in the play. Reela was sorta tall when she was eleven, jist like you. I'd imagine this dress will fit you fine. Well, stop standin'. Try it on."

Naomi ran to the bedroom and slipped off the faded cotton print that Mom had made for her last year. She lifted Reela's beautiful dress over her head and felt the supple, creamy crepe slide and cling its way down into a perfect fit. She stood before the mirror. Was it really Naomi Bradley standing there looking like a tall, slim angel child? What a perfect dress! Not one seam too loose, not one tear in it. Her hair fell across her shoulders touching the creamy cloth and blending into an array of gold, cream, and white tones as mellow and subtle as the paints in the picture done in oils that the principal kept in his office at school.

She walked back into the living room and stood just inside the doorway while Preacher Haller and her whole family looked. Preacher Haller smiled and let out a soft "Ah-h-h."

All Naomi's family was silent for a moment, then Paul said, "That's some hell of a dress. For cat's sake, that must've been made for a movie star or somethin'."

Naomi appreciated Preacher Haller's head shake when Paul cussed, but she liked what else Paul had said.

Benny and Bruce pulled at her hands and laughed happily. Dad started to bite on the tips of his reading glasses. "A golden willow. Now take it off so it don't git dirty. It ain't yourn. You hang it up till Sunday."

Ike and Pete and Jay teased and pushed, but it took no twisting at all to know their words were really compliments.

Mom said, "You heard your dad! Them dishes ain't doin' theirselves. Git that dress off and git busy."

Grace picked up Dad's newspaper, drew some crosses along the margin, and asked, "Anybody wanta play tick-tacktoe? Come on, Benny, I'll teach you. It's easy."

Preacher Haller was still full of fine smiles as he started telling everyone good-bye and invited them all out to the play at church. Naomi slipped back to the bedroom and took off the dress.

Mom waited for Preacher Haller to get all the way outside before she said, "It seems to me it's stretchin' the Gospel a bit to be puttin' on plays in a church house and stretchin' it a long way to be preachin' adornment by bringin' that dress over here for you to wear." That made the second time Mom had criticized Preacher Haller.

It was a little frightening to hear Mom talking like that, but Naomi must not allow her words to go deep enough to upset her. Nothing must keep her from wearing Reela's beautiful dress come Sunday.

On Sunday morning, Naomi waited for Grace to leave the bedroom. Even then she couldn't bring herself to put the dress on out on the open floor. She dressed in the closet, but left the door open so she could look across the room and see her reflection in the mirror, while no one could see her if they chanced to come into the bedroom. For a long time she stood looking across the room toward the mirror. The girl she saw reflected there was lovely. Imagine finding oneself pretty to look at!

She stepped out of the closet and gave a couple of twirls around the room and then quickly grabbed a thin, faded denim-patch quilt and wrapped it around her. The dress attracted attention like magic. She wouldn't be able to take that much attention. It was past the point of being natural.

Naomi ran to the pickup and jumped in with the rest of the family, who were all set for church.

Pete asked, "You cold, Naomi?" What y'wrapped up for?"

"No, I ain't cold. I jist don't wont to git Reela's dress dirty."

Grace plopped herself down on the tailgate of the truck, stuck out her chin, and said, "You're hidin'. I'd hide too, the way y'was showin' off in front of that mirror. You call that tryin' to act like an angel?" Grace saw everything. There were no secrets from Grace.

"It ain't wrong to play angel, or Preacher Haller wouldn'ta asked me."

"Go ahead and play angel! I hope y'die and turn into an angel jist like Aunt Wilma!" Grace folded her arms, scrambled to the side of the truck, and started to hum.

Naomi kept the quilt about her until she stepped inside the church door. Then she took it off, laid it across a chair, and let all eyes follow her as she walked to the front.

When Preacher Haller's little skit started, all Naomi had to do was stand there, being an angel in the beautiful dress. She did it real good, too. All the while the other players were saying things and acting out what the preacher had told them to do, Naomi stood up in Reela's dress and felt all the eyes in the congregation on her.

How strange that Preacher Haller did not know that clothes did count! People had never ever in her whole life drawn in a sharp breath when she'd passed them or nudged a neighbor, as they did now. People whispered, "Look, it's Naomi." Not "She's one of the Bradley girls" but "Naomi." What power there was in that dress! Why, there was no doubt she could be a mighty powerful woman preacher if she dressed the part.

She would wear beautiful clothes, and she would stalk up to the pulpit, and she'd preach God's words with power and force, and all the sinners in her congregation would come to the mourner's bench when she gave her call to repentance! The Lord would *have* to spare her to fulfill a calling so grand as that!

After the skit was over, she returned the dress to the Russels, but some of its power stayed with her, helping her see how it was going to be someday, when she was a great woman preacher.

She would stand up before her quiet and reverent congregation in one of her many lovely costumes. . . . Why, she'd wear a ballerina dress like that one on the girl in the big white art book at school. As she taught the Parable of the Sower, she'd be spinning and twirling, and when she came to the part in the sermon where it was time to ask everyone to take into account their own lives, she'd draw one leg up to touch her knee with the satin slipper and stand there all pretty and graceful like the pink flamingo bird on the fishing calendar in the hardware store. And when she told everyone about the life in the hereafter, she'd stick one leg way out in back while she stood on her toe with the other leg. And the very minute she called all sinners to the bench to repent, she'd do a grand split all the way down and bow her head and let her hair humbly touch the floor.

She was already pretty good at doing splits, and it'd sure be nice to be a preacher and dancer. Why, even Mom might learn to like a woman preaching if she saw it done right!

Grace came and stood above her.

Naomi hadn't realized that, while she was daydreaming,

she had actually done the splits, but there she was on the ground in a perfect split.

Grace pushed against Naomi's leg with some corncobs she'd been holding and said, "You think you're so smart 'cause you can do the splits with one leg back and the other forward, but let me see you do 'em with both legs goin' straight out to the side!" Grace pitched the cobs in the air, showing off by trying to juggle them. She thought she'd make Naomi look foolish by asking such a hard trick.

"You do it first and then I will," Naomi said.

Grace looked frustrated for a minute. It wasn't so easy to have to take her own dare. But Grace was a stubborn one. She started slowly inching her legs farther and farther apart, until at last her head jerked forward and down, and she did a somersault into the pile of chicken corn Naomi had shelled.

Naomi jumped out of the way. Gosh, that was a pretty fancy way to do a somersault!

But Grace went howling into the house yelling, "Mom, Naomi is doin' more of her nasty tricks!"

Grace was a tattletale, a big fat tattletale, spilling over with words, and not one word had she found to say about how good Naomi had been in the church play.

Naomi wished *Grace* would turn into an angel. Sometimes when Mom happened to have the teakettle up to full steam and had a minute to spare, she would run the comb through the steam and set Grace's hair in banana curls. Dad said it made Grace look like an angel.

Setting curls was one of Aunt Wilma's ways that Mom had picked up, though no one would tell her that out loud. Aunt Wilma had tried to curl Naomi's hair, but had given up with a playful laugh. "Naomi, it's hopeless! Look what a stringy mess I'm makin' out of you. Your hair's too much like mine. Mine never would curl, even if I wrapped it around a hot poker." But Aunt Wilma's hair was long and shiny and reached down almost to her knees, like the ballerina in the art book.

Naomi ran to the house and found the Sears catalog. On page 176 was a blue rayon taffeta dress filled with ruffles, a ballerina's dress. This year Naomi would be considered a full hand in the cotton field and would earn the money to buy her own clothes. Dad had said, "When you're big enough to buy your own clothes, you're big enough to choose your own clothes." With her own money she could have that ballerina dress! She could hardly wait for cotton-picking vacation.

Naomi watched eagerly the next day as Mom fixed her a cotton sack. It was made from Abe's old sack, which had worn thin from being dragged bulging with cotton through the muddy middles of the rows on bad days and over the sharp, dried cotton hulls on nice days. Mom had plenty of good canvas left to fold it over and seam it up short to the exact size for Naomi. She'd make that sack bulge again, stuffed full of cotton! Abe would like her in a blue ballerina dress.

It was great to be old enough to earn money! Money could buy lots of things: flower seed, for instance, if you wanted to have pretty flowers like Sarah Mitchell. But, that could come another year. She planned to work every year, year after year, and not be foolish with her money. God would help her become a rich woman and a powerful preacher, and He would be proud of her. Even Mom would be proud.

The day the picking started, Naomi ran into the field. She began picking so fast that she had to force herself to slow down just a bit to be able to guide the tips of her fingers' into the boll, just so, and avoid the sharp burrs as she pulled out the fluffy white cotton. Haste makes waste. She had to work hard, but she knew she'd better use common sense about it and make sure she was working well. She had to get the dollar fifty-nine it took for the ballerina dress.

She could hardly wait. First thing she'd do would be put it on and twirl until she got seasick! She'd fall over laughing and her head would keep spinning and she would feel strange and wonderful! In a week's time she'd be doing all that! The cotton wagon would get full fast on the first picking, and Dad would stop his work in the corn and take it to the gin and come right back with the money in his hand. By the end of the season she'd have lots of pretty clothes.

After she got the ballerina dress, maybe she'd get a pleated skirt to wear to school like the town girls did. When she played hopscotch, it'd show white and green and yellow plaid with every hop.

Her hands moved fast and faster. She might even buy herself some white furry shoes like the ones Abe gave Mabel Russel. That'd make everyone nudge somebody else and say, "Look, it's *Naomi!*" She'd smile at them, and her teeth would shine because she was going to buy some real toothpaste from Sears. If she didn't get all the money she needed by the time the cotton was picked over twice, she'd pull bolls. Lots of bolls! Ike and Jay and Pete and all the boys would see just how much she could do, and they'd never call her sissy or chase her away again. They'd say, "Naomi, that's a whoppin' sack of cotton y'got there."

Her hands were moving too fast; the burrs scratched her sweaty arms. Summer dresses and their short sleeves! It wasn't fair. The boys wore long-sleeve shirts in the field, and rolled them up at quitting time.

The sun was hot. She was getting tired already. She just had to take time to rest. Naomi lay backward on her sack for just a minute and used the lump of cotton she'd picked as her pillow. The sky sure looked pretty when you lay flat on a cotton sack and gazed straight up. That sun was bright enough to blind a man! Bet she could look straight at the sun and not go blind! She tried it for a second, but her eyes jerked shut. Anyway, the sun made the most beautiful pictures when you closed your eyes real tight; orange and red and pink blended in great feathery movements! The best pictures came just before one went to sleep. . . .

Suddenly, a sound! No, a smell. Cucumbers! Hs-s-s-s-s. Had to be a copperhead! Copperheads smelled like cucumbers. Naomi woke up fast, but the sting hit her leg all the same. Ripping the strap of the sack from her shoulder, she bolted and ran. The snake tumbled across the cotton row and started to wiggle away.

"Dad, Dad! A copperhead's killed me!"

Dad was way over in the cornfield! Oh, she'd never make it there! The house and Mom were closer. The sting was no worse than a little spider bite but Naomi knew she'd be dead if she didn't get help fast.

She stretched her legs farther and farther with each stride. Those legs had to obey. Dirty stinking copperhead! They were worse than rattlers. They never gave no warning.

She could hear screams from her brothers running behind her! Screams from Dad heading her way from across the field! Screams from Mom and Grace running to meet her from the house!

Mom caught her and screamed again, at Grace. "Go get Sarah Mitchell! Get her fast. Naomi is dyin'!"

It seemed to take only a second for the family to gather in from the fields. Dad stretched her out on the rough boards of the porch. He was giving orders in a powerful way, the words coming out low and strong and not at all like when he ordered you to get off a hoe handle and go back to work. Dad's orders were, "Ike! Hold down both her arms.

Jay, you and Paul hold her legs down, tight! I gotta cut. Pete, run and git that jug of coal oil off the back porch! Mom, get Benny and Bruce away from here. Hear me— move!"

What was that in Dad's hand? His straight-edge razor! He was going to use it on her. Naomi tried to run, but she couldn't move. The boys held on like leeches.

Dad's voice was calming her now. "It's all right, Willow. I've got to do it. Don't know anything else to do." A sharp pain, worse than when the copperhead bit, sprang from her leg as Dad made the slash. Again it came as Dad cut across in the other direction.

Pete, who was crying, moved in with the jug of coal oil and pressed it hard against her leg right over the cuts. Blood was dripping—she could feel it. Or was that coal oil?

She tried not to yell. She tried to lie still, but she couldn't. Oh gosh, they had to let her move. She couldn't stand it. Still, she didn't want to die—she had to cooperate. Aunt Wilma had died of a snakebite. Dad had used coal oil to save her too, but Aunt Wilma died, anyway.

Dad's voice was soft. "Hold on, Wilma, it's almost over. That coal oil's going to draw out that poison. It's got to. We don't want to lose you, girl. It's *got* to work!" Why did Dad call her Wilma? His hands were clutching her about the chest now, and he was shaking her and crying, "Don't die. Please, please don't die!"

Sarah Mitchell pulled Dad aside. "Mr. Bradley, let me. I have some serum that will help. Here, Naomi. It'll not hurt. Your sister Grace is a fast runner. Well done, Grace. Here, Mr. Bradley, let me. . . ."

Those were the last words Naomi heard for a while. When she awoke, there was Sarah Mitchell, a true nurse in a white smock, looking almost as pretty as Reela Russel and not acting a bit crazy. Her words came out in the slippery, clipping sound of a St. Louis accent, but they sounded beautiful, soft. "Naomi, Naomi. Wake up. You're all right."

Other people were hovering close by. There was Grace . . . and Paul and Ike and Jay and Pete. And down at the end of the bed—hey, who'd put her in bed?—were the twins.

Grace whispered, "I never wanted y'to die. I'm glad y'didn't die like Aunt Wilma did."

Dad came and touched her head. "You all right, Naomi?"

Paul said, "Pete put the cotton outa your sack into his'n. Weren't 'nough to weigh nohow."

Mom said, "Well, you're lucky you're not dead! You know better'n to sleep in a cotton row. You've been told a hundred times to look out for snakes. You was sent out there to work, not sleep. Now where's your clothes money comin' from? It wasn't worth my time to sew you up a sack, because you're likely not to be pickin' anymore this season. You don't git over a copperhead's bite so easy!"

Mom sounded like her natural self, but Naomi remembered that it was Mom who had first yelled for help for her.

Dad said to Mom, "Stop your frettin'. Sarah Mitchell said that medicine would have its effect and said we got no cause to worry. Said Naomi's heart was good. Hear that, Naomi? You got a strong constitution! It'd take a team of wild horses to kill this one."

Sarah Mitchell pushed back through to sponge Naomi's forehead, and the boys and Grace moved away to let her in. New faces appeared in the room, neighbors coming in to see her. She heard Mrs. Medlain say, "I had a sister die of a copperhead bite."

Mr. Curt Jackson said, "I got bit by a black widder spider, and they's deadly, but I come out of it."

Benny said, "I play with scorpions all the time, and they

are deadly as deadly can be and I ain't never been bit yet! Don't I, Bruce?"

Ike asked, "What part of the country were you in when you got bit by this black widder, Mr. Jackson? I never heard tell of a actual black widder bein' around here. And, Benny, them little lizards that folks call scorpions ain't no more a scorpion than a jackrabbit. I can prove it with my science book. Y'll see what a real scorpion's like."

Mrs. Jackson said, "Howdy, Naomi. Now, all you people, shet up sich talk. Do you feel like eatin' anythin', Naomi? I brought you a pie. I was bakin' pies for Curt when they brung the news. I ain't been bit by nothin' in my life nor had a sick day. Not a single solitary sick day."

Mrs. Kruse said, "I wish I could make the same claim. Sure wish I could. I'm tellin' you if it weren't for my morphine, I'd die of pain."

It was certainly nice having all the neighbors come calling just because of her. That had never happened before. But then she'd never been snake-bit before. As a matter of fact, she was the very first of all the children to ever have a snake bite. And she had survived it! Because of Sarah Mitchell, she had survived a copperhead bite. Now let Mrs. Jeno take the facts and still see if she wanted to call herself a fortune-teller. Naomi Bradley wasn't dead yet! The Lord had spared her for her calling.

Naomi tried to rise up on her elbow, but she was too weak. Then Sarah Mitchell, just like a lovely storybook lady, started gently moving people out of the room. She came back to lay her hand on Naomi's head. "Now go back to sleep. There, there."

Her smooth, cool hand, with no calluses, felt so soothing. Sleep. Oh, yes. The best pictures came just before one went to sleep. She saw herself take the beautiful dress from the Sears mail-order package. She'd show Abe and Preacher

Haller. "See my dress. Watch me twirl. Wanta see me twirl?"

She dreamed then that she was standing on a platform in a great church, like the Catholic church in a picture that Mary Jean Kruse had showed her, preaching a funeral for a dead woman in a glass casket. The woman wore a long ballerina dress and was Aunt Wilma. . . . No, no, it was Mrs. Jeno. The spitting image of Mrs. Jeno.

SIX

As Dad and the boys were leaving the breakfast table, Grace called to Dad and asked, "Couldn't y'git that woman preacher over near Bernie that Grandma Harney says has the gift of healin' to come bless Naomi? Mom says Naomi has got to be well before the hay balers come."

"Grace, I ain't gittin' no woman preacher now or never! Wouldn't let one set foot in my house. A woman's got no call to be preachin'. Ain't fittin'!"

Dad's words spoiled all Naomi's dreams, the dreams that had helped her heal and make progress, even if Mom did think it was too slow. Having a dream go so suddenly was too much. She cried out to Dad, "God likes it when His children preach His word!"

"Fiddlesticks! Get a hold of yourself, Willow. You still ailin'?"

Mom butted in with, "No, I don't think she's ailin' yet. I call it laziness."

"But what can a woman do to please God if she cain't preach?" Naomi didn't want Dad to hear Mom's words.

Mom said, "Well, lazyin' around ain't pleasin' to the Lord. Remember when Mary and Martha had Jesus to their

85

house. He let Mary know that a good woman does more than lazy around."

Dad pulled on his work jacket. "Naomi, it don't matter one bit what that preacher woman does with her life. As far as you girls is concerned, jist pattern after your mom. I'm sure the Lord is mighty pleased in a woman who works as hard as your mom."

Mom smiled, too pleased for words. Then, quick as a young kitten, she reached over to the windowsill and grabbed a book, *The Lionhunt,* and tossed it onto the dying ashes in the cookstove. "The Lord shore ain't goin' to be pleased with me if I allow that book in my house for another minute."

"No! No!" Naomi screamed. But already the flames were shooting up through and around the thin pages. "That's Sarah Mitchell's book. Dad, what'll I do?"

Mom answered for Dad. "Sarah Mitchell will learn what she can and cain't do in my house. There was naked black men in that book, naked as jaybirds, newborn. I said not a word when she brought in all those fancy flowers, puttin' high-falutin ideas in your head, but what this trash does to your mind is serious. Books have been the ruination of many a person!"

Dad said, "We'll have to settle it with Miss Mitchell one way or another. Why'd she give you that kinda book, Naomi?"

"Oh, Dad, it was a good book. It was about Africa, a country chuck full of strange things, and about this one great lion that no hunter could catch, one that wouldn't let himself git trapped. Now I'll never know . . ."

"Stop bawlin' now," said Dad. "Go take your mornin' nap. If you're goin' to git well before hay-balin' time, you better git your rest. Preacher Haller said he was plannin' to drop in to check up on you. Maybe he can help you calm down a bit. I got work to do. It cain't wait."

Mom waited until Dad got out the door to say, "Naomi, don't git any funny ideas that your dad tellin' you to pattern after me gives you any right to mess in my kitchen!"

Naomi didn't answer. She obediently went to bed to nap until Preacher Haller came. She could talk to Preacher Haller.

As soon as Preacher Haller arrived and got past the hellos to Mom and Grace and came to chat by Naomi's bedside, she asked, "What can I do? Dad won't let me take up preachin' and Mom won't let me cook and I hate peelin' potatoes! I gotta do something pleasin' before the Lord. I—I—I don't wanta die!"

"You ain't gonna die. You're lookin' almost well. Who says you got to cook to please the Lord? You know somethin'? Jesus came upon this very same problem. Remember the sisters, Martha and Mary, who Jesus visited? Well, Martha was puttin' all the emphasis on cookin' and Mary was wantin' to stay alongside of Jesus and listen to His stories. Know what He said? He said that cookin's not that all-fard important. Man has other needs than fillin' his belly. Ain't no sin in bein' a Mary. Here, here. Now stop that cryin'. Y'll be cookin' up a storm before y're old enough to marry anyway."

Naomi took Preacher Haller's comforting words and let them soothe her worries until he left and she had further time to think them over. It was a great comfort to have Jesus on her side.

But Mom thought Jesus was on *her* side! She and Preacher Haller had used the same Bible story to prove it. How could that be? Well, preachers knew more than mothers.

And that settled it. She would work in the fields like the Bible picture, "The Gleaners," which hung on the wall at school, and she could listen to the men's stories just like Mary listened to Jesus. She would learn all the things that men do in the fields, and Mom wouldn't have to worry if she was an old maid, for she'd be a help, not a burden. She would be a hard worker in the cotton, a hard driver of horses, and a hard plower of new ground, and—and she'd bale hay too! No woman ever helped bale hay. She most certainly would be well in time to help with the baling. Wouldn't God smile then? Why she'd live to be as old as Grandma Harney!

When the day finally came for hay baling, Naomi was as good as new and was one of the first out of bed and outside to greet the balers. They came with the sunrise, and if the weather favored them, they would stay until the sun set. Mrs. Jackson came along with her husband, not to work beside him in the field as was her custom, but to bake pies for the big feast.

"That's a thank-you job, and my specialty," said Mrs. Jackson. She patted Naomi on the back and said, "No copperhead could kill this one. Y're as good as new, girl. What thank-you job have you got up your sleeve? Y' should have seen the cake with red icing that Mary Jean Kruse made when we baled for them day before yesterday. Melted red hots colored that icing. M-m-m."

Grace shouted, "I git to fry the chicken. Mom's makin' light bread!"

Mom started building a fire beneath the wash kettle for heating chicken-scalding water. "It's too hot to start the cookstove yet. We got us a day ahead of us, all right. I set a good table for balers. I'm not like Mrs. Medlain, givin' them nothin' but fried potaters and beans! She deserved ever' bit of madness they showed her. Being busy with a houseful of kids ain't no excuse. Them balers ain't forgittin' it either!"

Mrs. Jackson nodded her head in agreement. "Mary Medlain made the mistake of lookin' on hay balin' as nothin' but hard work. No sich thang. It's that and more. It's the best of the harvest. Me and Curt's took in lots of corn, and it's slow and drug-out work. Two people in a wagon ain't no call to celebrate. But a group of happy balers, sweatin' and hungry— that's different!"

Mom stood up from her fire starting and looked all around. "Naomi, go find the twins! That's your job, to mind the twins today. I ain't got no time to be on the look-out for them, and I don't want them gittin' under foot, or worse yet, sneakin' out near them mowers."

That did it! Some thank-you job that was! Didn't Mom know that Bruce and Benny were six years old now and getting old enough to mind themselves? They'd have to, for she was helping Dad with the baling! She ran to the barn where Dad and Paul were fixing to leave with the last wagon.

Trying to act ordinary about it, she suggested to Dad, "Maybe I could help out with the balin'? Paul ain't much taller'n me. I can outchop him in the cotton field. I can . . ."

Dad seemed aggravated. "Naomi, git back in the house with the womenfolk where y'belong and help Mom out, y'hear?"

Paul rolled up his sleeve and made a muscle. Naomi tried the same. Dad wouldn't even look her way.

"Women in Bible times helped in the hay. There's a pic-ture—"

Dad was pointing at Bruce and Benny, who were leaning way over the horses' watering trough. "This ain't Bible times. Pay attention to right now. Git them twins outa that trough! You let 'em git soaked, and Mom'll give you the lickin' of your life, and it'll not be one whit more'n you de-serve! Git a move on; make yourself useful! It's a busy day, Naomi!"

It was a sin to argue with your father. She went toward Bruce and Benny. What right did those twins have even to be near the horses? They were too little to be allowed to hang out around the horses. Boys! Horses were for boys, even little boys with no muscles. Well, it was a girl in a beautiful ballerina dress who rode the horses in the big art book at school. Beautiful, powerful, graceful horses, and she rode them while standing on one leg!

"What're you doin' in the waterin' trough, anyway?" was all she said as she pulled the boys back down to solid ground.

Bruce looked at her, surprised, and lisped, "Makin' snakes outa horsehairs, that's what!"

Benny began reaching across the water again as he complained, "And—an-n-n-n' they got stole. Someone stole 'em and—an-n-n-n' we gotta find 'em 'cause six weeks ain't up yet."

Paul yelled, "A horse drunk 'em. Now git outa that water. Naomi, grab Benny!" She pulled Benny back to the ground again, but not before Dad had time to yell, "Naomi, y'ain't ever goin' to make a decent wife if y'cain't git kids to mind you."

Dad jumped onto the wagonbed next to Paul and rode off toward the hayfield. Naomi was left holding the twins. She refused to see Paul's smiling face. How could she ever get Dad to see her? To hear her?

Men didn't listen unless they wanted to. Someday, just after he'd had a big meal and the trainman had given him the *Kansas City Star,* maybe she could tell Dad about how Mom wouldn't let her in the kitchen. Maybe then he would forbid Mom to raise her voice against her daughter, just as he had done on behalf of Aunt Wilma.

Naomi kicked a tumblebug and made it lose its load. She'd already tried talking to Dad once, and hadn't gotten two words out before he said, "Naomi, cain't y'see when a man's tard? I been workin' steady for fourteen hours. Now let me have some peace and rest!" Anyway, she guessed talking about Mom was a sin. Had to be. Dad never had let her do it. "I ain't listenin' to no whinin'. Your Mom's a good woman, a hard worker."

The twins had grabbed her hands and were pulling, wanting to go back just once more to the watering trough. She turned them about and headed them toward the house.

Grace, Mom, and Mrs. Jackson were in the backyard. Three happy people. Mrs. Jackson had the usual strip of white lace down the front of her dress to make it look slimming. Mom was a big woman, but Mrs. Jackson was even larger. Big, solid, happy women, bustling about the steaming water from the wash kettle. Mom was heating the scalding water outside today because she wanted to make an early start. No one started the cookstove any earlier than necessary on a hot day. Dad said he could stand the heat, but just to hold that rain off until the baling was finished. Everybody was happy and excited today except Naomi. She held the burning torch under each chicken while Mom turned it to char off all the pin feathers.

"Take these in, Grace. You can start cuttin' 'em too. Me and Mrs. Jackson can finish up here. Naomi, you can git the twins to help y'roll the lemons. Jist keep an eye out so's they don't grab the knife, hear?"

If she couldn't get to cut and fry chicken, and if she couldn't go to the fields, and if she had to mind the twins, well, this would be the best way to do it. She'd take some lemonade to Jay. Jay loved lemonade. She looked at the happy little twins. They couldn't help being little any more than she could help being a girl.

"I hear," she called back. She took the twins to the back porch and immediately gave them each a lemon.

Benny said, "I cain't use my right hand. I got a splinter."

Naomi stopped to remove the splinter. "That's a bad sore, Benny, but now it's well." She kissed his finger, then put a lemon in his left hand and started both twins rolling lemons back and forth, back and forth, across the clean oilcloth that covered the old worktable. She grabbed a lemon in each of her own hands and started working with them.

"You got strong hands, Naomi," Bruce lisped, and he smiled.

She started letting herself go and began to enjoy the lemons. Wow! Did they smell good! Once a year, at the most twice, they got to have lemonade. But no matter how long it was since the last time she never forgot that wonderful smell, clean and sharp. Her mouth watered for the taste treat to come.

As soon as the lemons felt soft and gave easily to each squeeze, she sliced them and dropped the juicy slices into the big five-gallon crockery churn.

Grace came to smell and inspect them, then had the nerve to ask, "Mom, can I add the water and sugar?"

Mom gave a busy nod, and Grace poured. The twins tasted it and made stiff, tart little faces to match the lemons. Mom wiped her hands on her apron and came over to add the exact amount. When satisfied, she said, "Naomi, put in the ice."

Okay, she liked getting the ice, and when she got the lemonade all ready, she'd go to the field and help bale hay yet.

Naomi got the block of ice from the cool, damp shade under the milk trough. Dad had brought back fifty pounds from the ice house in town last night, and it had lasted extra well. Not even half melted. Mom had told Dad to buy a box of tea too. Dad called it a luxury. Naomi called it puke.

She got the ice pick down from the porch rafter and cracked the ice into chunks to be used equally to cool the lemonade and the iced tea. There was no sense to wasting good ice on that icky tea, but Mom and some of the men loved it.

Bruce and Benny scampered to collect the slivers of ice as they flew off. She put half in the churn and reluctantly left the rest in the stewer pot for the tea. Then she walked to the kitchen and swiped a piece of pie dough that Mrs. Jackson was rolling and flipping around.

Mrs. Jackson smiled and flipped her a little extra piece and said, "How's my girl that a snake couldn't kill?" She kept rolling out pie dough at a fast pace.

"I'm fine, Mrs. Jackson. How you gonna make that funny piece fit a round pan?"

One piece of pie dough wasn't working just right. Mrs. Jackson ripped off a piece from one corner and, with a thud, thud, thud, pressed it into a gap in another spot. "There, that oughta fix it. Thangs don't always work out right the first time around, but sometimes a little patchin'll do the trick."

Mom's voice called out, "Naomi! Take them twins outa the kitchen!" Mom heard and saw everything even if she was managing five different jobs on the other side of the kitchen. Mom added, "I guess y'could set them boys playin' right outside the kitchen winder. Mrs. Jackson could keep her eye on 'em. What with all the pies she's got to make yet, she'll be there a while. Then you could take a jug of water out to the workin' folks. They'll welcome it."

Working folks? Why, everyone was working. Oh, well . . . "Mom, Dad would love to have a drink of lemonade. He likes the way you sweeten it. He always likes to get the first drink of lemonade."

Mom paused for only a second. "Okay, fill the jug."

Grace raced ahead of Naomi, sloshing precious lemonade all over! How dumb of her to try to fill the jug straight from the gourd dipper used in the water bucket. Grace could be awful clumsy.

"Try usin' a funnel, Grace." Naomi moved Grace aside so she could place the funnel into the narrow neck of the jug.

Grace refused to move, which made Naomi trip and almost upset the big churn. Grace laughed and said, "Clumsy!

Sometimes, you're awful clumsy, Naomi. I better help y'carry that jug to the field. Mom! Can I help carry the jug to the field?"

Mom said, "I don't care, Grace, soon's your last skillet of chicken is turned. One more turn, and it'll be ready to rest in its juices on the back of the stove and get done through and through. If there's one thing I cain't abide, it's half-done chicken. And, Naomi, while she's doin' that, you add a few more potaters to that bucketful y'peeled last night. . . . Watch them peels!"

Naomi added five more potatoes. On the last one she made the whole peel spiral off and then threw it over her shoulder. Just as she was checking to see what letter it made, so that she would know the initial of her future husband, Mom caught her and scolded her.

"Pick it up, Naomi, and put it in the slop. Not much use you wonderin' what his initials'll be. When you go out to the field now, you better keep a sharp eye on how field work's done, 'cause you're never goin' to catch a man with potater peelin's that thick. Little wonder y'got done so fast. No man could afford to have you in a kitchen. Well, both of you, git goin'. Time's awastin', and me and Mrs. Jackson has things under hand now. Let me know what the men's got to say about that lemonade."

Naomi let Mom's words trail off. She was happy to be allowed out in the hayfields, and she intended to keep an eye open as to how it was done. She'd taken the men jugs of water other years and she loved being out in the open fields, loved the smells. And this was a day for smells! Her hands brushed near her face; she could still get a strong whiff of lemon.

The air was full and rich with the pungent smell from the fresh-mowed oats. Nothing in the whole world smelled as great as oat hay, fresh made. A hot day made smells stand out like that. The pokeweed along the field road drooped in the heat, and she could feel the sun beating into her scalp. Her legs were sweaty and the grass cut against them. Girls had to accept a few scratches. She'd never wear men's pants like some of the town women did to protect themselves when they came out to pick cotton. The Bible was strict against women wearing men's clothes.

Naomi could see the hay rake working a distance behind the mowing machine in the middle of the oat field. The baler sat between the two patches ready to bind the whole stalks of the partially matured oat plant into moist food for the horses this winter. The hayrack, which was full of bales, would meet Pete on his way to the barn.

"How about a drink?" he called.

"Y'll have to stop over near the baler. I'm 'sposed to take it to Dad first." She could beat Pete chopping cotton too, and there was nothing to driving a team of horses with a wagonload of hay. Let Grace look. . . . Hey, Grace was gone! Now where had she run off to so fast?

Grace was over near where Jay was running the mowing machine, moving around and around the field. He now had it down to a small square about three hundred feet across. Naomi knew why Grace had gone over there. She walked quickly over to the persimmon tree that stood in the oat field, set the jug down in the shade, and ran to catch up with Grace.

That little patch of oats still standing would be alive with scared rabbits that had been going toward the middle ever since the cutting started. Pretty soon they would start to run out to find new places to hide. That was the time to start chasing them.

A good runner could catch a nice frying-size rabbit, whack its head on the ground, and bring it home for supper. Pete and Paul used to wait for the chase and always brought home at least two rabbits. Just wait until Naomi caught two. Then Dad would see what great things she could do, and he'd probably start begging her to help bale hay.

Grace was after a rabbit already, but she'd never get it. Jay would roust out another one pretty soon. But Grace quickly dashed in front of Naomi across the stubble. The rabbit hardly had time to know he was being chased before she had caught it, killed it, and started after another. Well, let her try to get another, thought Naomi. She'd never make it. Paul said a person had to be long-winded to get a second rabbit.

Jay was tightening the circle now. Five or six rabbits ran out in all directions. One came within two feet of Naomi before it bolted to take a new direction. She tried to grab him as he turned but missed. She never took her eyes off him as she began the chase. Around the field they went. When he headed for open ground, she forced him back in toward Jay and the mower. Around and around the little patch of remaining oats she ran, always just behind the rabbit, never getting closer, never lagging behind. Salty sweat dripped into her panting mouth and past her eyes onto her nose. She would never give up.

Jay had the patch finished now and several rabbits joined Naomi's in the mad, crazy running, but she never once lost sight of her own rabbit. He would be getting tired soon, and she didn't want to lose him and have to start on a fresh runner. Right through the midst of the other rabbits she ran. Once she almost tripped on Grace sitting on the ground. So Grace had given up. Too short-winded.

Jay was yelling, "Hang on, Naomi, y'almost have him!"

Back near the mower she chased and on into the field, twice around the persimmon tree. She'd grab him. She'd grab him with both hands. She was gaining. She was sure she was gaining!

Naomi was tired, but she was getting closer and closer.

The big gray cottontail circled back near Grace. Oh, it was getting hard to breathe. She had to get him now or never.

Naomi fell forward. Gasping sounds filled the air, sounds from her own throat. No matter, on that last lunge she had caught the rabbit! She could feel him in her hands squirming against her chest as she lay there facedown on the ground. She had her rabbit!

Grace yelled, "Have you been chasing that one rabbit all this time? Ye gads, y'want to drop dead or something? Mrs. Jeno said y'd die before you were fourteen, and now I know it! I was winded a long time ago, and I got better breathin' than you!" Grace was standing over her, still shouting. "Where'd I lay my other rabbit? Jay, did y'see where I laid my other rabbit?"

Naomi tried to pull her tired muscles up to standing, but she fell right back down again. The rabbit kicked wildly in her hands. He had to be as tired as she was, but he was still fighting. She let her fingers relax their hold. She felt the sudden jerk before the frightened rabbit ran away. Her own tired body relaxed.

"What in the creation?" Grace yelled.

Naomi couldn't answer. She lay on her stomach now, crying, and she didn't know why.

"I couldn't do it! I couldn't beat his brains out!"

She saw that Grace did not understand. She turned her face back to the ground and moaned. Mom wouldn't understand. Dad wouldn't either. She had no rabbits to show him and she was glad . . . and sad . . . and angry, too.

Grace was yelling again. "Now that beats anythin' I ever seen. You run longer than any human bein' should be able to, and then you let that good fryer go loose. D'you think it was a pet? Rabbits are food!"

Naomi knew that. She guessed she knew that. She watched Grace go back home with two rabbits. Grace would tell about her losing the rabbit, and Mom and Dad would be disgusted. She got up slowly, walked away from Jay, over to the persimmon tree to sit down. She didn't want the men to see her now, not even with the lemonade jug.

The persimmons on the tree were still green and would be puckery until frost hit them, but she cracked a seed to see what shape she would find at its heart: a knife, fork, or spoon. A spoon. She cracked some more: just spoons. A knife meant you were going to marry a handsome man; a fork meant you'd marry a rich one; a spoon meant . . . it was just an old persimmon.

Nobody would want a girl who couldn't cook, couldn't work the fields, and couldn't kill a chicken or a rabbit. She threw the nasty old persimmon away. Her puckery mouth made her feel ugly. She picked up the jug and went toward the balers, who'd been waving her over to them for a good five minutes. She had planned to greet Dad with prize rabbits as well as a cool drink but . . .

"Give me that jug! We're all dyin' of thirst!" Paul called. "What's in the jug? It don't look like water."

"Lemonade. I made it myself, and Dad gets the first drink."

Paul laid his baling wire down on a knotted-up sack. "Wow! Lemonade!" He grabbed the jug. "A man needs a drink after all that work." Before Naomi could make him wait his turn, he had swung the jug up with one arm and drunk a big gulp of her wonderful lemonade.

At first a wild look hit him. He sat the jug down, clapped his hands to his mouth, and began coughing and sputtering and grabbing at his stomach with his other hand. Naomi watched until he settled down enough to yell, "Naomi, you'd better run. I'm goin' to hit you even if you are a girl. I mean it, Dad! She's tryin' to poison us all puttin' coal oil in that rotten lemonade!" He was coming toward her and she ran.

Coal oil? It must have been that blamed funnel! Someone had put the funnel that was used to fill the lamps on the wrong nail! She hadn't noticed the smell, so it couldn't have been much, but a little coal oil taste could go a long way. Words, threats, shouts came cutting through to her. She not only had made the men do without, she'd wasted all that money for lemons and ice too. She glanced back and saw tired, sweaty, thirsty men, with God-in-Heaven roars coming from their mouths.

She ran, ran across the new-mown fields and deep into the corn patch. The sharp, long, crisp corn leaves cut across her face. She sat down. No use running anymore. She was winded. She hadn't really recovered from chasing rabbits. Anyway, a criminal had once hidden in a cornfield for thirty days and no one had found him.

Naomi lay on her stomach in the corn row. Mom had warned her many times about getting a man riled, and she had riled all the balers! She lay there for a good long while, but finally her fear gave way to hunger. She remembered something else Mom always said: good food soothes a man. If Dad was soothed, and if there was company all around, she might not get punished. She had escaped punishment before when there was a lot of company, or when it was Christmas or Easter, or when Mom was awfully busy, though in the latter cases she merely got the punishment postponed. It seemed safest to go back right now if she ever planned to go back.

As she walked homeward across the stubbles, a mama killdeer went flopping on an angle in front of her and crying as if her wing were broken. Naomi walked in the direction from which the bird had come to look at her young ones. The bird's fuss became louder.

Naomi smiled and said to the bird, "Oh, stop your actin'. Go play your tricks on someone else. I ain't no snake. I wouldn' t ever hurt your babies." Killdeers were sure smart birds, putting on a show like that. "You're a good mother,

and I know it ain't easy when your nest is on the ground.
But you found a way. You're smarter than me. I never found
no way to help bale hay, but I gotta find a way to keep them
from gettin' even and Dad from killin' me."

She made herself walk on. As she got near the house,
she could see Grace by the woodpile, cleaning her rabbits.
Naomi stopped to watch. Grace carefully cut just behind the
ears and then took the tip of the knife and circled each leg
at the middle joint. The skin slipped off neatly just like
a pullover sweater. Grace looked so pleased with her work.
She took the fur and stretched it around a couple of flat
boards and laid them on top of the chicken house to dry.
Grace would make a good wife, it was plain to see. Any
man would be glad to have Grace.

Naomi heard noises from the men. They were coming in.
She quickly scooted past Grace into the enclosed back porch.
Quickly she began helping Mrs. Jackson peel onions for the
mashed-potato salad. She was still breathing hard. She
tried to control it by asking Mrs. Jackson slow, calm questions. "Y'think this'll be enough onions? Y'wont me to add
the mustard?"

Grace came in proudly, telling Mom about the rabbits
and about her great chase to get them. Usually when Grace
told of her own accomplishments, Mom would ask, "And
what was Naomi doin' all this time?" but Mom was too
busy now, with the noise of the men getting closer, to make
talk.

Naomi looked about for a hiding place. The cotton sheet
that now neatly covered the worktable hung all the way to
the floor. On top sat twelve pies that Mrs. Jackson had
finished, five green-tomato mincemeat and five lemon cream,
and near the edge two large blackberry cobblers made in
high-sided bread pans. How lovely they were. Mrs. Jackson
was an artist! Naomi felt so hungry.

The men were at the pumphouse now. She could hear the

pump being primed. At last they'd quench their great thirst and wash away the sweat and dirt and heat. That would help. She hoped.

Grace called from the kitchen, "Naomi, go out to the pumphouse and bring in my rabbits so's them balers don't git dirty water all over 'em!"

She didn't answer Grace nor move. She hoped those men would get some soothing food in them before they noticed her. The men always ate first and then went out to rest under the shade trees while the women ate. Right now she was glad that girls ate last.

Grace was calling again. If Grace didn't keep her mouth shut, she'd be in for it, for sure. Dad and Paul and two of the other balers were coming through the door. Naomi kept her back turned and kept working over the potato salad, making flowers on top out of sliced hard-boiled eggs. Mom would scream at such wastefulness, but she had to make this job last.

Grace's loud voice came from the doorway now. "Naomi, now you git my rabbits in the kitchen. I said I don't wont them gettin' dirty. Now if I have to leave this chicken and it burns—"

Paul was the first one in. He held the cleaned rabbits high in the air in front of Grace, who grabbed them and ran for the kitchen. Paul was a help sometimes.

For a moment Naomi had forgotten that Grace was not her problem but Paul. She tried to duck under the table-cloth, but Paul had seen her and held his foot on the bottom of the long sheet so she couldn't get under. It caused the two long cobbler pies to tip and start to fall. Naomi grabbed for them and managed to knock one into the other as she caught them. "Now look what y've done, Paul. Mom'll kill you. What a waste! What a waste!"

"Poison the lemonade with coal oil, will you?" Paul swung at her and the pies.

101

Mom was at them at once, trying to break up the fight and shouting and screaming. Suddenly Mom stopped scolding and said, "Now, Paul, you cut out your scufflin'. Look at all these nice vittles we got ready and waitin'. Naomi couldn't help no little mistake. Naomi, take them cobblers in and dish them out in saucers. No one will even know the difference."

What? Mom taking her side? Mom had *never* been kind and considerate like this. Then she noticed that Mom held a funnel in her hand and was sneaking it down to the nail that hung above the coal-oil can. So it was Mom who had stuck the wrong funnel on that nail above the worktable!

Mom went on talking in an unnatural, kind voice. "Now cut out your feisty ways. Take the men in and git them set down. Naomi, git on and take care of them cobblers."

Paul looked at Naomi with his brow knotted, like when he was going to call someone a cuss word. Then he stuck his finger into a cobbler, tasted it, and turned to obey Mom and go.

Mom kept talking as she hustled through the door. "Grace, you know better'n to bring these rabbits in to me right now when I'm at my busiest. Git 'em in salt water, save 'em for supper."

Grace showed her catch to Dad and whoever else would look and listen to her. Naomi scooped up the cobbler and tried to think how she could get this unexpected turn of events to work more in her favor.

Dad said, "Getting two rabbits is mighty good for one girl. Honestly, I do believe some girls could be traded for a couple of boys and call the slate clean. Now you girls git along, and you men move right on in there to the table." The men moved along, and Dad stopped just for a second to say to Mom in a whisper, "I told y'before to watch where you hung that coal-oil funnel."

Mom was aggravated. "I was tard last night. I've been

workin' my fingers to the bones. . . ." Dad walked away from Mom. Then, making a smile come back to his face, he went in to settle at the table with the rest of the balers.

Naomi gave a big sigh of relief. Suddenly, a large pair of hands cupped over her eyes! A deep, mean voice said, "I've come to arrest you!" For only a second was Naomi frightened. She knew who it was.

Either Benny or Bruce yelled, "What you arrestin' her fur?"

Chet White began laughing and pulled his hands away from Naomi's eyes. "Oh, I don't know," he said. "What've y'done wrong, Naomi? Well, that's what I'm arrestin' you for." The men all laughed, and Naomi knew it was all over.

"I guess I made a mistake and got a lot of people mad at me."

"That's all right, Naomi. You're tryin'. Jist remember. Nobody ever kicks a dead dog."

Mr. Kruse said, "I do declare, young lady, y' shore got understandin' parents. My old man would've tanned my hide off if I'd pulled a caper like that'n when I was a boy!" Naomi couldn't imagine that big red-necked Mr. Kruse had ever been a boy, or that anyone had ever, ever given him a licking.

"Mine too," added Mr. Jackson, forcing his barrel belly between the table and the cane-bottom chair, which was pressed against the wall now that two tables were joined together. "Naomi is goin' to be the spittin' image of her Aunt Wilma in a few more years. It don't hurt none to be purty does it, honey? She's a right nice looker, Mr. Bradley."

Naomi felt a little uneasy about others calling her pretty. The last time that had happened was when she had worn a pretty dress, and look what had followed that—a snake had bitten her.

Dad bit off the piece of fried chicken he held, and as he

chewed hard, he said, "I cain't say that looks is so all-fard important in a woman. The first test I'd give to a woman is to see if she had calluses on her hands. I don't know that what comes by nature is so great. Willingness to work is what counts!" Naomi wished Dad hadn't acted so disappointed in the fact that someone did think she was pretty.

Mr. Jackson wiggled his chair around just a bit more before he answered Dad's remarks. "I got nothin' against a hard worker. Lord knows, I got one of the hardest workin' women there is. It's a compliment I meant when I said y'got a good-lookin' daughter. And your sister was a good-lookin' woman too."

"Looks don't mean ever'thang! Wilma never married," Mom put in.

Dad was plainly annoyed with the line of talk and was eating his chicken too fast, as if trying to keep more words from coming.

Mr. Jackson said, "Now maybe I know something that the rest of you don't know. That fortune-teller in Poplar Bluff told Wilma she'd never marry. It had nothin' to do with her looks. But it's my belief that her dyin' had. That woman was too purty to live. It's sad but true."

Dad slapped down his chicken bone. "She died because she was bit by a water moccasin!"

Mom whispered to Mrs. Jackson loud enough for Naomi to hear clearly, "She died because she was a burden."

Mrs. Jackson said, "Some thangs in life is worse than dyin'. Looks can git a girl into trouble as well as bein' somethin' to raise a man to complimentin'." Naomi understood what Mrs. Jackson meant. Faith Jackson was pretty, and she'd turned out bad. Mr. Jackson ought to watch his words or this wonderful hay-baling dinner might not be so wonderful yet.

Mr. Jackson's voice got calmer and calmer as he said,

"Sorry, Mr. Bradley, we all know how she died. Sorry. We know you tried all you could to save her. I meant nothin' against my wife. A man cain't ask for more if he's got a hard-workin' wife. And believe me, I got one. She does the work of two men. Fine worker. So's your wife. Could be Naomi here will take after your wife. Children don't always take after the one they look like. Not always."

Grace stood in the dining-room doorway and rubbed the calluses on her hands. Naomi went to the back porch and picked up a whole mincemeat pie. She went out to the back yard to eat, think, and watch the horses. The muscles of the tired animals rippled as they pawed the ground nervously. A sweaty horse was a beautiful sight. She sat there watching until the men came back out to go to the field, and she knew it was time to do dishes.

When she got back inside the house, Mrs. Jackson and Mom and Grace were still crunching their chicken bones, sucking the marrow and eating the gristle, and talking about how well the dinner had come off. No one had missed her.

It took her most of the rest of the afternoon to do up all the dishes, what with stopping to chase Benny and Bruce. Mom and Mrs. Jackson took a walk through the garden, to discuss their canning. Grace went out to chase rabbits again in another oat patch. She wanted another rabbit, and she'd most likely get it. Dad would probably let Grace bale hay if she asked, but Grace didn't want to bale hay.

Jay wound up the last area of oats and came back to the house with Grace. Grace was carrying something. It wasn't a rabbit. It was a chicken!

Jay was laughing. "Go on in, Grace," he said. "Show Mom your rabbit." Then he noticed Naomi and said, "Thanks, Naomi, for not giving me any of that lemonade."

Grace called to Mom, "Jay cut a chicken's leg off and had to kill it."

Mom answered, "Well, scald it and pick it. We'll add it to

the rabbits for supper. Too bad we cain't save the lot for another day. It's a shame to have all this good eatin' in one day. But your Dad says he likes good eatin' for supper, too, on hay-balin' day, and a man's likes is his law."

Give a man what he likes. Food soothes a man. Naomi was setting a plan. Like Mrs. Jackson with her pie dough, if things didn't work out just as planned the first time around, with a little fixing, one could . . .

When suppertime came, Dad ate with as much relish as he had at noon. "A body never gits tard of good eatin'. We've worked off ever' ounce we ate at dinner. These boys make real field hands. Times like today is when a man feels right good about havin' boys."

Grace said, "You like my rabbit?" Dad smiled a complacent approval.

Benny and Bruce fought over the chicken wishbone, and the other boys laughed and bragged. No scolding. All were happy.

Naomi ate slowly, her head bowed, thinking, waiting for the right time. If she couldn't work for Dad, then she'd make Dad work for her. She'd have her thank-you work yet. She knew Dad didn't ever plan to embarrass Mom by telling whose fault it was really that the lemonade had coal oil in it, and there was no chance at all Mom would ever mention it again. She asked Dad, "Don't you think Mom ought to let me practice more at cookin'? I wouldn't ever want to turn out something bad like that lemonade again." She felt as crafty as a killdeer bird as she said it.

"Y' better not!" Paul said as he jumped up with a doubled fist. Everybody was agreeing at once that Naomi sure needed cooking lessons. Jay said, "I cain't think of anythang Naomi needs more'n cookin' lessons. Y' hold on there, Naomi girl."

Dad said, "Well, Mom, how about it? I think you ought to be helpin' her learn before she goes and gets married not knowin'." This made the boys all start laughing and teasing, and Mom start to chew a little faster. Mom wouldn't refuse Dad.

Mom said, "I'll teach her what it means to work in a kitchen! I'll not have it be said that a girl was turned out of my house without knowing the value of hard work! If she don't turn out right, it'll be because of who she patterns after and no fault of mine!"

It didn't matter how she said it, the important fact was, Mom had said it! And tomorrow, when Naomi was helping cook, she just might watch them potato peelings too. With a little more attention to the matter, she'd likely be able to get those peels paper thin! She'd get so good at cooking that neighbors would flock in just to taste it and to look at it, for she'd see to it that her pies would be even prettier than Mrs. Jackson's. And she'd smile as she sat and watched people go look in her slop bucket just to check to see if she really made a potato peel as thin as rumor had it that she could! She'd be the hardest worker ever in the kitchen for a long time to come, because God, being a man, would surely be soothed seeing her such a good cook.

SEVEN

After a time Mom finally kept her word and let Naomi begin to learn to cook. Mom *never* went back on her word to Dad or God. So now Naomi was making a whole dishpan full of mashed potato salad in honor of Abe being home for two weeks. Abe had got the horse! But he had had to pay twenty dollars instead of fifteen because Queenie was exceptional. That was what Abe said, and no one argued against his saying it. She was black, as black and shiny as a newly broken piece of coal dropped from the freight train.

It was a joy to fix dinner for Abe. With the wide, flat blade of a case knife, she smoothed the huge mound of mustard-yellowed potatoes into a perfect hill. In the center of the hill she planted a whole green onion. It was supposed to be a tree, a palm tree like in *The Lionhunt*. On the right side of the tree she sprinkled pieces of green onion blades, finely chopped. That was the grass. She made the grass curve and wave until it looked like a shoreline. Now what could make a boat? One big pickle split made two ships. She got three little boats by carving one carrot. Seashells, she needed seashells. She crumbled some bacon around the shore. Pretty good, but— She broke off some bits of eggshell—perfect! She'd warn everyone not to eat the eggshell part.

"Grace! Grace, come here. See? Well, ain't it beautiful? Thank Abe'll like it? It's purtier than the mashed-potato salad that Preacher Haller's mother brings to the church dinner, ain't it? She just puts a radish in the center and slices boiled eggs on top. Well, do y'like it?"

Grace was staring. She was impressed. Why didn't she say something?

"Well, do y'like it or don't you?"

"Mom! Mom! Come see what Naomi's done this time."

Mom ran in and stood in front of the worktable and glared for several long seconds before she grabbed the onion from the center. "That does it! You're worse than Wilma. Worse, I tell you. 'Cause of your Dad I been holdin' my tongue, but there's a limit. First y'breaded pork belly with cornmeal like Mrs. Kruse—oh, don't thank I don't know who you copied—and your Dad bragged it up. I said nary a word. Nor did I when y' put sugar in the cornbread so's it'd shine on the crust. We want *bread* with our beans, not cake!"

"I ain't wasted nothin', Mom. I made sure I didn't waste nothin'."

"So y' ain't been wastin'? Well, what do you call havin' chocolate gravy ever' single solitary mornin' for breakfast! The chocolate's already used up for the whole month! Bacon-grease gravy is ever'day fare. You'll let it go rancid at the rate you're goin', and that's wastefulness! Out! Git outa my kitchen!" Mom was using the side of her broad hand to sweep together the grass and boats and seashells, and then, cupping her hand, she scooped them up and over the side of the table into the slop bucket.

Naomi ran out toward the chicken house to be alone. She didn't think she was going to cry, but if she was going to, she wanted to get to the chicken house.

She never made it all the way, for Pete was sitting behind the smokehouse and *he* was crying.

"Are you cryin', Pete?"

Pete blew his nose. "No, I ain't cryin'. I ain't ever cried in my life!"

"You have too, Pete, and you know it. And I thank maybe y'been cryin' now. What's the matter with you anyway?"

"You wouldn't understand. You don't have to fight Paul all the time and always lose."

"I have to fight Mom. She ain't gonna let me cook no more."

Pete was sitting up straight now, and in the sunlight the little white hairs on his face shone golden and made him look as if he were starting to be a man. His voice changed from sad to mad as he said, "Well, some things are impossible! Paul's born with bigger hands than me, and I cain't beat him at pickin' cotton. I've tried and tried, and I just cain't do it."

Dad and Paul were coming in from the barn, and Dad caught Pete's last words.

"What is this y're sayin'? What cain't y'do? Pete, a body can do anythin' they set their mind to. Hear me? Now set your mind to it and stop frettin'."

Paul stuck his hands in the front pockets of his jeans and strutted around. *"I* can do anything I damn well want to do."

Pete jumped up and doubled his fist. "So can I! Put up your fist, Paul. I could outpick you, outswim you, outride you—just name it. I could do any of those things if I pleased. But I don't please. I'm going my way and you go yourn, or else put up your fist!"

Dad started walking away from the boys. Naomi joined him. She might as well go into the house alongside Dad. It'd be easier that way. She had to go back in sometime, anyway. Besides, she liked what Dad had just said.

"Dad, do y'thank I could do anythin' I set my mind to, too?"

"Sure, Willow, sure y'can."

"Okay. I thank I'll learn to swim."

"Now, Willow, them ditches ain't hardly the place for a young lady to hang out. What y'need to swim for?"

"I might drown if the truck turned over in a ditch someday. It might if y'hit a bump on Seven Ditch bridge, where there ain't no railin', and had a wreck right on the bridge and the truck plopped in the water. I'd drown."

"Naomi, run along. You got an imagination a mile long and two miles wide. I ain't that kind of driver no way."

Mom had been standing by the stove listening. She said, "Go fur the milk crock in the pumphouse and git it to the table, Naomi. Forgit the swimmin'. I ain't havin' no daughter of mine hangin' out around a bunch of naked boys on a ditch dump! Girls don't need to know how to swim. I don't."

Naomi didn't say anything more. No use pointing out that every woman in the books she read knew how to swim. Mom would just say she wasn't to pattern after book women. Naomi went about her chores and did her own thinking for the rest of the evening. God would provide. There would be something she could do that was special and acceptable.

At the supper table Abe said he liked the insides of the potato salad. She'd known he would.

After Naomi finished the supper dishes, she went out and sat on the edge of the horse trough to watch Abe break Queenie so she'd be able to pull a plow. Queenie was a beautiful-enough horse for riding, every bit as pretty as any horse in any book, but Abe needed Queenie for plowing too. He wanted to marry Mabel Russel and start his own farm.

"You watching how this is done, Naomi, case y'ever

112

wanta break a horse?" Abe was good-natured in his teasing. He didn't really mind Naomi watching, and she knew it.

First Abe got Queenie used to the halter, then to having a bit in her mouth, and finally he tied to the hamestraps a singletree, the thick wooden crossbar that was a guide for the reins when hooked to the plow. But it was getting too dark to take Queenie for a run with the things all hooked up.

"Well, how am I doin', Naomi? Wanta come watch me take her out in the mornin'?"

"If y'don't start too early. Mom won't let me out till I do the dishes."

Abe slapped her on the back. "Well, work fast and come join me soon's y'can. I gotta git an early start. My time's short. I aim to hook on Ike's old snow sled for a drag behind her tomorrow. It'll slide fine in the mud." Ike's sled was about four feet wide with two big wooden runners sticking out from under. If Queenie could pull that heavy thing, she could pull a plow.

The next morning Dad woke everyone up by calling, "Pete, Ike, Paul, Jay—you too, Abe—all of y'come. We're goin' over and set that blasted pump for Faith Jackson. We gotta fill in the well too, so the kids won't fall in, and that'll take ever' one of you."

No one seemed very happy about it. For once Pete and Paul were grumbling about the same thing, and Ike and Jay had had other plans. Abe was grumbling, "Dad I just got one more week b'fore I gotta go back to my job. I may as well forget about marryin' if I don't git Queenie broke."

"Abe, when y're home y'll work with the family. No one wants to do this job, but the preacher assigned it to us. If we all join in on it, we'll git it done in a couple of hours or so. It won't hurt you to give us a hand."

Mom was poking the wood into the cook stove. "How

come Preacher Haller's gittin' fard up about helpin' that no-account woman. She's as big as a growed man and eighteen years old if she's a day. Let her mind them kids and they won't fall into the well. I growed up 'round a well and never drowned! A body could poke Faith down that well, and there'd be no loss felt."

Mom wasn't seeing the whole story. A pump was more practical in a lot of ways. It'd save Faith Jackson from having to use a draw bucket, and besides that, whoever heard of lizards getting into a pump? It was a known fact that lizards infested Faith Jackson's well. That was why Donny and Billy got so many boils.

Abe and the boys put on jackets and were on their way to the truck, when Dad said, "Paul, git out to the barn and drop some feed down to the horses. A man cain't totally neglect his own place for the sake of a neighbor, whether a preacher requests it or not."

After the others left, Naomi told Paul, "I'll drop that feed down. I gotta climb in the hayloft to gather eggs anyway." Paul didn't argue.

Naomi had wanted to get another close look at Queenie, and this was the best way. She put on Paul's old kneeboots and started wading through the mire out to the barn. The manure smell rose stronger with each squishy step. She could manage barn chores as well as the boys. Better, in fact. Somebody had left a lantern burning all night. Wasteful, but Dad never yelled.

Queenie nickered.

"I'll get you oats in a minute. Stop your fussin'. I got to get the eggs first."

Naomi climbed the ladder to the hayloft and took five eggs out of the hen's nest and put them into the little pouch she'd made by knotting up the tail of her skirt about one hand. She clutched the skirt tightly and started back down the ladder, holding on with her free hand. Boy, mud on one's boots sure could make going down a ladder a slippery job. Oops! Both feet slipped! Naomi grabbed with her egg-holding hand. She looked down to try to anchor her feet on the ladder. Four broken and splattered eggs hung dripping from the ladder rungs. Below, one still lay whole in the soft manure. Wasteful! Wasteful! Wasteful! She'd better never let Mom find out.

Naomi slopped mud up over the broken eggs. Mom would never know. Sometimes hens laid eggs and sometimes they didn't. She picked up the one good egg and put it on the fencepost. She'd wash it and take it in as soon as she fed the horses.

First she went into old Turner's stall and fed him. Then she opened the door to Queenie's stall to give her her feed. There was no point in dropping the feed from the hayloft. She didn't want to climb that ladder again. Besides, she liked to get close to horses. Queenie trembled just a bit and blew warm air toward her.

"It's all right there, beauty. I ain't goin' to hurt you. Now here's you some nice oats." The big horse continued to tremble and to dance around just a bit, and then she settled enough to take a mouthful of oats.

"Why, you're about the nicest horse I've ever seen. There ain't no use in Abe worryin' about breakin' you. I bet you could pull a plow right now."

Naomi wanted to do an important job, one important enough to impress anyone, even God. It wasn't as if she had actually planned on doing it. She didn't remember setting her mind to it. She simply started carrying things out a step at a time.

She kept talking and talking, and Queenie kept listening and shaking just a little. Queenie did give a good-sized jerk when Naomi slipped the bit in her mouth and the bridle over her ears, but Naomi talked her calm again. Things were going quite well until Naomi tried to tie the singletree. "Now behave yourself, Queenie. You gotta let me tie this on. Abe says all wild horses gotta get used to pullin' somethin' simple first before they try out a real plow. There now, let me grab the reins and we'll get y'out to where Ike's sled is."

It must have been the noise the singletree made. Queenie bolted. That jerk about knocked Naomi over. It was all she could do to hang on to the end of the reins.

That Queenie could run like a wild one. Naomi hung on to the reins and Queenie kept on running. Across the soupy barn lot and down the sloshy mud road she went. Queenie didn't let anything slow her down. Naomi felt her feet lift out of the kneeboots—they were too heavy with caked mud anyway—but she still hung on. Now that was silly. Abe had said, "Always let loose and let a new one run if things got out of control." She sailed past the mulberry tree, whose branches formed a giant umbrella. She'd have to let go. But she was in the air most of the time, it'd be awful to let go.

She'd have to do it. She started to loosen her grip. But just then she spotted Faith Jackson's little boy Billy walking on the road ahead of her, never once looking back. She clung on tighter than ever! She couldn't let go now. Queenie'd slam right into Billy Jackson. Naomi's dress was ripping as she pulled to try to make Queenie move to the right, away from Billy. Oh, dear God! Billy, Billy!

Naomi yelled and bellowed, but Billy didn't get out of the way. Oh, Lord a mercy! Billy was going to get killed! She pulled the reins to the right with all her might, harder than she knew was possible. Her body hurt! Her arms! Oh, she was dead herself! Great pain matched the blackness that settled in to ease it.

The next thing she heard was Mom's voice sounding distant and hollow: "Now, Benny, maybe she ain't goin' to die. Y'heard Dr. Foster say she's got a chance." Then she felt

Mom's hand touching her forehead and heard her sobbing, "There, there, honey."

Good gosh, Mom must think she was dying. Mom had never ever called her honey in her whole life.

Lots of voices were buzzing and humming. "Bad, bad. She's real bad." "Mrs. Jeno prophesied it. Oh, Lord!" "She was a good girl."

Then a new voice: "What happened to her? Anyone know?"

Faith Jackson's voice answered loud and important. "I seen. I'll tell you what happened. There's my poor little Billy walkin' down the road right ahead of that wild horse and not movin' to the left or right. I'm yellin' but I'm too far away for him to hear. Then I start wishin' for him to feel my carin' and move. 'Feel! Billy!' I yell, but he jist don't. And then I sees Naomi a leanin' hard to one side of them reins, tryin' to make that big wild horse change its path. And she done it! Oh, thank the good Lord, she done it! The horse goes runnin' past Billy free as nature herself. Then I sees Naomi alayin' there and my Billy comin' back and tryin' to get her to set up—him tryin' to help like that and nothin' but a babe in arms hisself. I woulda gone to help, too, but I figgered I best git Naomi's pa. So I did. I seen him asailin' to his pickup and splittin' mud as he made that truck head home.

"Well, I kept my head. I'd heard on the party line this mornin' that Dr. Foster was out to Mrs. Russel's 'cause of her havin' another nervous breakdown on account of Reela runnin' off with that city man. I lit out to the phone and called the doctor there. I'll bet it weren't ten minutes till Dr. Foster was here! I want ever'body to hear it. I take it as a sign from the Lord, my Billy bein' saved, and I feel His lovin' grace and I accept it. Praise the Lord! I'm a changed woman!"

"Amen! Amen! Glory be!" It was like a revival meeting

there in the bedroom. From way out toward the front porch came Mrs. Jackson's voice. "Hallelujah! Hallelujah! Faith, come let me see you, and bring them grandbabies out here. Let me touch my grandbabies."

Naomi tried to open her eyes to see faces, but giant eyelashes stood like bars on the window of a jail before her.

Ike said, "Naomi shoulda let go. A runaway horse could jerk a man's arm right off."

Jay said, "Naomi never let go of anythin' she didn't want to."

Grace whispered, "Naomi did lots of good thangs too."

Grace always spoke nice about the dead! But Dad was saying, "I never said she didn't, did I? I said she knowed better'n to mess with that wild mare. I ain't figgered out yet how a slip of a girl got that harness on her. Why, Abe planned on feedin' that mare from a chute for the next month. Blame kid never hears a word a body says!"

Abe said, "Animals sense when a person is afraid. Smell them or somethin' like that. Queenie jist knowed Naomi wasn't scared. That's got to be the only explanation."

Mr. Jackson asked, "What are you goin' to do with that mean horse, Abe? I wouldn't work him. My Aunt Johnnie got mad at a cow that was mean, and she kicked her. Never milked her again, and this was when her family needed food in a bad way too."

Benny cried, "Naomi's got blood all over her dress!"

Grace said, "It ain't noticeable. Her dress has red flowers in it." Then, saddening her voice again, Grace went on with her good talking. "Naomi was good to me once at Christmas. She was a good person."

Mom said, "I admit she was good in her way. She took the blame last summer about the coal-oil lemonade when it was me that hung that funnel where it oughtn't be. I coulda let her learn to swim. She wanted to awful bad. Now it's too late. Oh, Lord!"

Benny said, "Naomi knew how to preach the best funerals for woolly worms."

Bruce interrupted with, "Sarah Mitchell's standin' at the front door, and the whole yard's full of people!"

Paul started talking in a quiet, sad voice, as if Bruce hadn't said a word. "Yeah, it's a fact. Naomi had a tender spot. She couldn't kill a thang if her life depended on it."

That did it, Paul getting teary. Naomi made her throat muscles work. "Watch what you're sayin'. I can hear ever' one of you."

Benny started crying louder. Bruce was saying, "How can she hear with her eyes closed?"

Dr. Foster pulled an eyelid way back, farther than necessary, and said, "She's coming around. She made it! Well, I guess I'll git on back to the Russels' before her other two girls bring on a relapse. Sarah's here. You won't be needin' me anymore."

Dr. Foster gave instructions to Sarah and left. Dad yelled a few words to folks in the yard and asked them all in. Naomi got her voice under control and her eyes open. What was the matter with her arms? They were thickly bandaged.

There stood Sarah Mitchell in a regular dress just like a regular woman. Her brown hair was mussed. She must have run all the way from her house. Sarah Mitchell said, "What's this I hear about you saving little Billy Jackson's life? That's a wonderful thing you've done, Naomi."

"Gettin' myself half kilt? Y'call that wonderful? I'm jist a girl and don't know how to handle horses. I never did get to hook on the sled. And now my arms are ruined. I'll never learn how to swim. I'll never amount to anythang."

"Naomi, when a person risks her life to save the life of another, that's something wonderful. I think we'll all agree that you already amount to quite a lot."

Paul said, "Yeah, she saved the life of Faith Jackson's kid, and Faith wouldn't go out of her way to—to do one damn thang for—"

Dad said, "Watch your words or I'll have Mom give you a little talk on manners. A repentant sinner deserves respect. Miss Mitchell, did Dr. Foster tell y'jist what all is wrong?"

"He did. She'll have to keep these shoulders wrapped so those pulled muscles get a chance to heal. She's a very lucky girl, but she'll not be able to be up and about for a while. I'll drop by every day that I can, as I go my rounds."

Dad said, "We'd appreciate it. Naomi ain't hardly got over that snakebite good, and I jist don't know if Mom can manage her bein' down bad agin. I'll git you a dozen eggs if y'can use 'em. It was our chickens what ruined your flower bed last week. Never knowed of chickens driftin' that far from home before."

Sarah Mitchell shushed him. "I'll not need eggs, but I'd appreciate it if you repair my flower bed. As for Naomi, these muscles will be back to normal one of these days, and she'll be a strong, reliant girl yet. Of course, not using the muscles will cause some atrophy, and later on I'll give her some special exercises to help restore them. I think swimming might be the best therapy."

It was said! And from the mouth of a real nurse. Naomi looked Sarah Mitchell right in the eye and said, "Sarah Mitchell, I like you. Why, you ain't crazy at all."

Sarah Mitchell smiled. Too bad Sarah Mitchell was not an acceptable woman to pattern after.

Mrs. Jackson pushed in close. "Naomi honey, you done me the best turn a body could've done this day. You not only saved my grandbaby, but you give me back my Faith. If I can ever do you a turn, let me know. I'm sendin' y'over a pie tomorrer. Now you rest up and mind Miss Mitchell. They say accidents come in threes, and you've had two mighty close calls, so take care. Y' hear me, little lady? Take care."

EIGHT

"Honor thy father and thy mother: that thy days may be long upon the land . . ." She had obeyed. For one terrible long year she had obeyed, but she was dying anyway. For a few short weeks Sarah Mitchell had taken Naomi along to the swimming hole, where they visited and splashed about and played to make her arms strong again, but after that it was nothing but obedience and work and misery. The minute Mom thought Naomi was capable of work once more, she chased Sarah Mitchell away, on the grounds that Sarah had had a baby out of wedlock way back when she first came to Missouri's swampland. Naomi didn't believe that story, but Grace did.

Dad had given Naomi the chance to decide whether she was well enough to work or whether she still needed Sarah's physical therapy. It was hard to do, but at the time she had been brave and honest with herself and Dad, and had admitted that she was indeed well. She hadn't spoken to Sarah Mitchell since—Mom's orders.

There had been no third accident, and so no reason to call on Sarah, but now Naomi had to see Sarah Mitchell. Honestly. This was worse than an accident. When she got up that morning, Naomi had discovered sure signs that she was dying of cancer. For sure it was cancer, the same as Mrs. Jackson was dying with, and she needed a nurse. She sure wasn't going to let Dr. Foster, a man, examine her. Preacher Haller had said that nurses and doctors were often tools in the Lord's hands and that if people died anyway, then it must be the will of the Lord. No one should question the will of the Lord, he said.

All the same, Mrs. Jeno had prophesied that Mrs. Jackson would get skinny and die, and now it was happening. All the things Mrs. Jeno had predicted were happening!

But why would the Lord will Naomi to be dead? People said Mrs. Jackson had lived to see Faith straighten out and that she had been rewarded enough on this earth by that alone, but Naomi was still waiting for the big things in her life, for her big mission. Why hadn't the Lord made her days long upon the earth as a reward for her obedience? She had obeyed Mom by not speaking to Sarah, obeyed Dad by working hard in the cottonfield. She could outchop Paul and outpick Pete.

Naomi had stayed in the field so much that it was hard to keep her skin white. She'd worn long black socks and long-sleeved black blouses and had fought the cotton burs and berry stickers until there were so many holes in her clothes that she looked more like a bird dog than old Spot. Dad could check her hands anytime and find calluses: calluses on her palms from chopping cotton, on her fingers from picking, and even on her shoulders from the strap of the cotton sack. Naomi pulled her hands up out of the dishwater and held them as if she were showing Dad her calluses. Did they make a girl good or keep her from dying?

Her body ached with the misery of death that was upon her. She needed a woman she could talk to in a very private way. She must see Sarah Mitchell! It meant disobeying

Mom, which was against the Scriptures, but if she was dying anyway, what good would the Scriptures do?

"Naomi, answer me!" Mom yelled from the back porch. "If I have to call you jist one more time, you'll wish you had. Hear me?"

Naomi walked out to see what Mom wanted.

"Wash them fruit jars. Your hands is the skinniest in the lot. They'll go in easier. Git them jars clean, or there's no use cannin' these peaches. They'll spoil in a dirty jar." Mom was cutting peaches. Grace was peeling.

Lined up along the wall of the closed-in back porch were nearly a hundred dirty fruit jars. Naomi filled two galvanized washtubs with water. In one she tossed a couple of hunks of lye soap; the other she left clear for rinse water.

"Mom, why'd y'buy peaches when our own trees bore fine this year?"

"The peach peddler offered me these bruised ones for thirty-five cents a bushel. Lots of 'em I'll can. The others'll make good peach butter. Likely Abe and Mabel'll need some, just startin' out married life. It's a mountain of work, though. Don't know how I'll git time out to set with poor Mrs. Jackson."

Grace said, *"Mr.* Jackson'll jist have to set with her hisself. Y'cain't possibly go with all this many peaches, Mom."

"Curt Jackson ain't fit to set with her! Last time he took a turn was the time he told her Dr. Foster said she was dyin' of cancer. Dr. Foster oughtn't never 've trusted that 'un to keep a closed mouth or a Christian attitude. He cain't even git his crop in without her there to help him! Lordy, I oughta lay down this knife and do my Christian duty and go set with her."

Naomi knew how Mrs. Jackson must feel, knowing for sure she was dying. It was awful to be alone with the knowledge of your own death. "I'll go, Mom. I'll set in your place. I know how to fix her pillows. I watched you do it."

Mom stopped slicing peaches and looked toward Naomi for a long time. "Yes, you go. I made my pledge at church to set whatever hours is needed ever Tuesday and Thursday afternoon, and I'll keep it. It's all in the family. Go ahead. I need Grace here to peel, but soon's you git them jars clean, you go ahead."

Before Naomi had the jars half finished, she knew what else she'd do. Sarah Mitchell went to see Mrs. Jackson every day. She would quickly run over and ask Sarah Mitchell if she couldn't meet her at the end of the lane and ride over to the Jacksons'. Dad had had a phone put in after the last accident, but if she used that, everyone in the county would soon know Naomi's secret from the party line. Maybe on the way to the Jacksons' she'd get a chance to ask Sarah about her problem.

It wasn't easy to call on a person you hadn't talked to for almost a whole year and ask for a ride. But Sarah didn't act as if it had been long at all. She seemed as cheerful and warm and close as if their last visit had been only yesterday. It was good to see Sarah again, and Naomi realized how deeply she had missed her. It wasn't just the talk she'd missed, it was the laughter and the playful splashing of water, the whole joyful thing of being with Sarah. She felt that she hadn't really laughed for a year. Now, of course, there would be nothing to laugh about.

Naomi changed her dress and hurried to the end of the lane and waited for Sarah's little coupe to arrive. At last a cloud of dust whirled around the corner and there was Sarah.

"Hop in, Naomi, I'm running late." Sarah's face was glowing with friendliness. "Gee, it's good to see you again! I haven't had one decent excuse to go swimming since we last went. Nor has there been anyone I'd care to go with, just for fun. Now tell me how you've been. Bring me up to date, Naomi."

"I'm fine." Naomi tried to smile to match Sarah's cheerfulness. It was awfully hard to smile when you were dying.

"Well, how are your arms? How are things at home? Tell me, just how did you get your mother's permission to come along with me. I'm delighted!"

"Mom's cannin'. She'd rather have Grace help her with the actual cannin', and she let me go as soon as I had all the fruit jars washed. You probably know how the church women is takin' turns settin' with Mrs. Jackson. Today's Mom's turn, but she cain't go or all them bruised peaches would spoil. You ought to see that little peach tree you ordered for me. It's got three peaches on it already, and it's such a young thing, and they're the biggest peaches I ever saw."

"As big as the picture in the catalog? I'd love to see them if you think your Mom wouldn't mind."

"She'd mind. She don't actually know I'm with you. She jist gave me leave to set with Mrs. Jackson. She don't know how I'm gittin' there."

"Will it cause you trouble?"

"I decided I was ready to risk that." She would wait until later to tell Sarah that to a dying person certain risks are not important anymore.

Sarah's brown hair blew back behind her ears as air surged in through the open windows. What a pretty woman Sarah Mitchell was. What a wonder that she never had a beau. Sarah smiled again. "Anyway, I'm glad you're here. How long do you want to be at Mrs. Jackson's?"

"Three hours or however long it takes. That's what Mom is signed up for, and it lets Granny Hakasen catch a nap. I never even knowed that Mrs. Jackson had a mother until she got sick and Granny Hakasen come up from Arkansas. Folks say she is pushin' eighty herself, and she's a real saint the way she spends all them long pitiful hours settin' beside her daughter, waitin' for her to die." Sadness filled

Naomi as she talked. Could Sarah sense it? Could Sarah know that not too long from now someone would have to be setting with Naomi?

"I know Granny. She's a trouper all right, and Faith's been a lot of help too until the last three weeks. Her baby is due any minute, did you know that? Smile a little, Naomi. Look on the good side of things. Isn't it nice that Faith is back in the good graces of her parents at a time like this? Wouldn't it be much sadder if you hadn't brought them back together?"

"I reckon. Grace told me that Mr. Jackson didn't make up with Faith that time at the runaway. It ain't all my credit, some goes to Chet White. Mr. Jackson didn't let her actually come back home to visit until she and Chet White got married and give Billy and Donny a real last name."

Naomi said no more for a long while, and neither did Sarah. Naomi wished she could come right out and tell Sarah about herself, but there was no opportunity to start the talk flowing.

Finally Sarah said, "Naomi, you don't act like your old happy self. It's really hit you about Mrs. Jackson, hasn't it? I can't let myself think about it too much, or I'd never be able to make my rounds. Thank God for morphine. Cancer is a bitter killer."

Big tears moved in as Naomi sobbed. "Yes, I know."

"Come on now, Naomi. If you're going to be a help you have to keep your chin up. Sometimes it can even help us when we're forced to witness suffering. Did you know that? Did you know it often fills me with gratitude for life when I see how fragile life is?"

Again sobs gave way. "Yes, I know." She mustn't do this to Sarah. Sarah was trying to help her, and she wasn't cooperating. She pulled in the next sob and tried to talk naturally. "Mom said almost the same thing, only backwards. She said that me and Grace needed to see sufferin' so that we'd keep check on the state of our own souls, for life was fleetin' and—" Naomi couldn't talk normally anymore so she didn't talk at all for a while. Sarah had said that cancer was a bitter killer. What kind of help was that to her to hear such talk?

"Sarah, ain't there a thing Dr. Foster can do to save Mrs. Jackson? Everyone in the county talks about the sadness of it. There ought to be at least somethin' to try."

"Maybe someday, Naomi, but nothing now. We need a lot more time for research. Dr. Foster has done all he can."

"I sure don't thank Dr. Foster had any business tellin' Mr. Jackson that his wife would die! Now why did he do it? Didn't he know that Mr. Jackson would turn right around and tell Mrs. Jackson?"

"Just a minute, Naomi. I don't think Dr. Foster believed Mr. Jackson would break a confidence, and for that matter neither did I. It's normal for a doctor to tell the family in a case like this."

"Well, even Mom wouldn'ta told Mr. Jackson. Mom says it's ruined Mrs. Jackson. She used to lay there and tell Mom how she planned to plant her potatoes in the wane of the moon next year so's they wouldn't all turn to vine, and stuff like that, and now she don't hardly talk at all!"

"Dr. Foster did what he thought was proper, and even the experts don't agree what that is. Anyway, what happened is not directly related to Dr. Foster, but is a matter between Mr. Jackson and his wife. And I'm not passing judgment on him, Naomi."

"Judge not, that ye be not judged." That was Scripture. It didn't pay to argue a point with Sarah Mitchell. She didn't even go to church, yet she knew Scripture.

Sarah waited a little bit, and Naomi let her wait. She didn't plan to argue anymore. That wasn't what she'd come to do. Sarah reached out a hand and touched Naomi. "Mrs. Jackson sort of knew, anyway. She'd already made funeral arrangements."

"Sorta knowin' and knowin' is two different things. She made them funeral arrangements jist in case, for Mr. Jackson cain't handle stuff like that. Mom says Mr. Jackson jist naturally poured all his burdens on his wife, and this was no exception. Dad agrees that Mr. Jackson is a pretty sorry man, not respectin' a dyin' woman's feelin's!" Naomi didn't know why she was shouting at Sarah Mitchell or why it felt so good to do it. She added, "And they're not judgin'!"

Sarah Mitchell closed her lips. This was the first fight Naomi had ever had with Sarah Mitchell. She had turned a good friend away from herself when she needed a friend the most.

"Well, Naomi, we're here. Try to keep your voice down when we go in. We wouldn't want to upset Mrs. Jackson, would we?"

How could Sarah talk like that? How could she think for one minute that— The car had stopped in front of a three-room house sitting on a little rise of sandy soil. Mr. Jackson came out, wearing faded overalls covered with several large neat patches of darker blue material. Mrs. Jackson had taken the patches off the back part of other worn-out overall legs. Wonder who'd patch his overalls now?

Mr. Jackson said, "I'm not goin' out in the field this mornin'. She's takin' on somethin' awful. I think this may be her last day."

Sarah Mitchell took out her black bag and walked into the front room. She spoke in a low but exasperated voice to Mr. Jackson. "Dr. Foster told you that it takes time. This may or may not be her last day. Try not to let her hear you say things like that, Mr. Jackson. We don't want to add to her suffering, do we? It'd be best. . . ."

Mr. Jackson's face began to turn a deep red. He wasn't a

big man, except for his belly, but he had the red-faced look of a big man from living out in the field a good share of his life. His face was getting redder still as he snapped, nice and loud, "Ever'body's tellin' me what's best. My wife wonts to know! No one's got no right to accuse me of talkin' outta line. After her cousins come down from Michigan, she knew it weren't jist bursitis and a bad stomach, like Dr. Foster told her! She can put two and two together! She said to me—" Mr. Jackson's voice turned quiet and weepy. Muscles tightened in his short neck. "She said right out, 'Curt, me and you's never kept no secrets. Tell me if I'm gonna die.' I told her, like she asked me to do. She wonted me to tell her the truth. Them's her very words, 'Tell me the truth, Curt' is exactly what she said."

Seemed like everyone was yelling at Sarah. Naomi began to feel sorry for having yelled at her good friend.

Sarah said, "I know, Mr. Jackson. I'm not accusing you. I'm just saying, let's be careful what we say in front of her."

Granny Hakasen came out to greet them. "You're a welcome sight. My girlie needs you. I'm 'most worn out—tard and weary as a lame fox tryin' to keep up with the pack. I ain't et yet. I declare I'll feel better soon's I git me a little molasses in me. Dr. Foster wont let me have no more sugar, so's I cain't eat my oats. I don't like oats with no sugar, so I settle for molasses. Glad y'came, Naomi honey."

Naomi followed Sarah and Mr. Jackson into the bedroom where Mrs. Jackson lay. She *was* getting skinny as a rail! Mrs. Jeno's prophecy had come to pass! Now Mr. Jackson would have to know Mrs. Jeno had the gift.

Mrs. Jackson was trying to move to invite Sarah and Naomi into her room. "I'm sorry we had to hurry you, Miss Mitchell, but it's gettin' almost more'n I can stand. I'm sorry to act like a baby. I've always been strong and could stand a lot, couldn't I, Curt?"

Mr. Jackson said, "That's a fact. She's always made a better hand in the field than any two men. I'm goin' to miss her. And strong? Why, remember that time she got that superstrength and toted her whole dresser right out of our burnin' house?"

Why couldn't Mr. Jackson stop his talking? This wasn't a company visit. It wasn't the time to spin tales or recall bygone times.

When you looked at frail, skinny Mrs. Jackson, it was hard to believe that once she had carried a big dresser all alone, or that she'd once gotten in a rowboat during floodwaters, and single-handedly took feed to all the stranded cattle. The cattle had gone to the high ground of the ditch dump in back of Naomi's house for safety. Every day, until the waters settled and the cows could return home, Naomi had stood at the window and watched Mrs. Jackson empty a boatful of feed for them. Mrs. Jackson had once brought along a rifle and shot the rabbits that had also taken refuge on the ditch dump! She ground the rabbit meat up with some salt pork and made sausage enough to keep her family in meat the rest of the season. Mrs. Jackson was a provider, all right, a hard worker. But the Lord hadn't added much to her years. Could it be that Abe was wrong when he said the Lord adds to your number of days if you're good? But that was questioning the Lord's will.

Mrs. Jackson said, "Miss Mitchell, I got every'thang ready. I talked to Mr. Crenshaw again when he came over yesterday, and it's all set. He'll get his undertakin' fee from my burial policy, and we made arrangements to git the cheapest casket so's there'll be enough from the policy left over to pay at least twenty-five dollars to Dr. Foster. You tell him that. Naomi, tell your ma she can use my flowers out in back of the house to make wreaths if she wonts to. Curt don't mind, and they'll all be dead shortly anyway. And

Preacher Haller's promised me that he'd have some of the church women come in and finish my cannin' so's I don't have to worry 'bout Curt havin' food this winter."

"Mrs. Jackson, it's all right. Now don't talk so much. Naomi, help me change these sheets. I'm sorry to have to make you wait for the morphine, Mrs. Jackson, but we need your cooperation just a little moment until we get these sheets changed." Naomi helped Sarah do everything that she was told to do and then tried to prop up all the little pillows and tuck quilts in and around to help support Mrs. Jackson's sore body.

Mrs. Jackson said, "I got to git ever'thang settled. I got to talk whiles there's still time."

But she stopped talking and began crying.

Naomi didn't blame Mrs. Jackson for crying. She felt like crying herself. Poor Mrs. Jackson, not getting to live to see the new baby.

Mrs. Jackson moaned. "I'm sorry. I've always worked. Oh, Lord, take me!" It was cruel to have to see a woman with the sure knowledge of death about her. That knowledge filled a body with fear, squeezing out every ounce of faith they once had. If Naomi were a doctor, she'd go to court and have a law made that anyone, fortune-tellers included, who told another person they were going to die would have to submit to the terrible torture themselves. And the judge would bang the gavel hard on the desk and shout, "Take them to the dungeon, and tell them they have exactly one hour to live, and let them see how they like it!"

Sarah nudged her out of her thoughts. "Naomi, help me with the spread, will you? Faith has certainly managed to get these sheets nice and white. You've a considerate daughter, Mrs. Jackson, and she'll be a help to your husband too, so don't worry about that."

"I never wanted to be a burden to nobody. Curt never

had to pay a cent on doctor bills for me, but now . . .
And the pain . . . Why don't He take me? I jist cain't bear
it. Why am I havin' to suffer like this? What have I done?"

"Heaven is sweeter to those who've known suffering,"
Sarah said.

The pain left Mrs. Jackson's face for a moment. A thin
smile came across her lips, and she said, "Then I'm headin'
for the sweetest heaven y'could imagine. Sweet Jesus, sweet
Jesus."

Sarah Mitchell gave Mrs. Jackson the morphine, and her
taut body relaxed. A little hope went a long way. It wasn't
just Sarah Mitchell's medicine, it was her words too. Being
a nurse was a nice job, a helpful job.

Sarah said, "Naomi, I must go on over to see Mrs. Russel;
she's real bad again. A nervous breakdown is serious too. I'll
be back for you after a bit."

Mr. Jackson went on out to the field, after all. Naomi sat
and watched Mrs. Jackson as she slept.

Finally Mrs. Jackson awoke and whispered, "Where is
ever'body? Did I die, Lord?"

"Is there anythang special you wont me to do, Mrs. Jackson? If Faith's baby comes, don't you worry who'll wash
them sheets instead of Faith. I'll do it." As a rule, Naomi
hated washing big sheets on the board, but somehow this
was different. It wasn't work, it was helping.

"Yes, Naomi, I got somethin' I need done. Y're a school-
girl, and I hear you write right purty. Git me that there
book settin' on the shelf."

Naomi reached for the lone book that sat among a row of
carnival trophies and little homemade doilies on a rough
board shelf tacked on the wall at the far end of the bedroom.
The book was gray and the edges were worn and frayed,
but the name *Pollyanna* could still be distinguished on the
faded cover.

"Open it and write inside, 'To Faith, my daughter. With love, Momma.' " Mrs. Jackson began to cry again. "I oughta've talked more of love to Faith. I'd planned to do more of it soon's I got up and around." Tears kept back her words for a minute. "That's sich a good book. I never got past third grade, but I could read that book right well. There was many the time, when I was low, it was my savin' grace. It's mine to give if I like. Anyway, Curt wouldn't mind a bit; he ain't never been one to read. That looks purty, Naomi. You wrote it jist the way I wonted it wrote."

"If you want me to take it to Faith, I will, Mrs. Jackson. Me and Sarah Mitchell's goin' over to see how she's gittin' along."

"Thank you, Naomi, and tell your ma thanks for lettin' you come. Tell Faith, I love . . ." And the tears and sobs came fast and cut off her words.

All Naomi could think to do was to reach for Mrs. Jackson's hand and hold it. For a long while she stood there until she realized that Sarah Mitchell had returned and had her other hand. Mrs. Jackson was asleep. She let Sarah lead her out of the Jacksons' house toward their next call.

Naomi sighed and settled into the car seat. "I'm glad someone invented morphine. It's a blessin', ain't it?"

Sarah just looked at her for a moment. Then slowly she began to explain. "Yes, Naomi, it is in Mrs. Jackson's case. It's a miracle to ease her pain. But morphine can be terrible too. Did you know Mrs. Kruse has taken it for years for low back pain? She's so dependent on morphine now that she can't even get up to do her housework without it." Sarah remained silent again for a while, then continued. "Last week they started enforcing the law against selling it from the drugstores, and she's going mad without it. I don't know what to do for her. I guess I'd better stop by. Dr. Foster can't give morphine to anyone just to keep an addiction going. That's what hurts a nurse most, when she can't do *anything* to help."

All at once Naomi remembered that she was the patient and Sarah Mitchell was the nurse she had come to for help. She felt anew her own low-back pains where cancer was eating away at her insides. How was it that she could forget her own cancer while she was taking care of Mrs. Jackson?

But now they were at Mary Jean Kruse's house. Naomi didn't know what she'd say to Mary Jean. She had never been over here when things were bad. Grace said that Mr. Kruse had been on the party line for a couple of days trying to call long distance somewhere to locate a priest, but without success. Grace didn't know why he wanted one, and she didn't dare ask and let Mr. Kruse know she'd been listening.

Preacher Haller's Ford was parked in the front yard at the Kruses, right beside the grape arbor. The old farmhouse looked almost like the barn, except that it had a long porch. Mary Jean and her three little brothers sat on one end of the porch. Coming from the house were loud curses and pleadings from Mrs. Kruse. Naomi and Sarah Mitchell walked up to the door, but Naomi didn't want to go inside. She'd never heard a woman curse in her entire life. Sarah Mitchell pulled her hand and led her in through the front room, on past the kitchen table with its fancy padded benches covered with blue-and-white oilcloth, and then to a small back bedroom next to the kitchen pantry.

A stifling smell of vomit and urine greeted them as Sarah opened the door. There was Mrs. Kruse, wearing a crumpled, dirty green velvet dress, her lovely red hair a stringy mess as she whipped her head from side to side in vomit, and screamed and swore. She was bound to the bed by ropes. She couldn't move her arms or legs. Preacher Haller knelt beside the bed, his highly polished boots touching the mud-

134

covered work shoes of Mr. Kruse, who knelt beside him. They were both praying out loud.

Soon Preacher Haller sounded a loud amen, and Mr. Kruse said one in echo. Then Preacher Haller laid his hands on Mrs. Kruse's head and said, "In the name of the Lord, Mrs. Kruse, I bless you, that this demon will go away and you can find peace from your naggin' wants."

Naomi tripped on an ash-wood chip that had been used to replace a bed castor. Mr. Kruse looked up and saw her and Sarah. "I tried to git her priest," he said, "but weren't no use tryin'. He's travelin'. There ain't enough Catholics around, and he's not likely to be found. I had to git someone. I had to do somethin'. She put on her purtiest dress and was afixin' to take off walkin', I don't know where to. I had to tie her down. She's out of her mind. I had to do somethin' to help her! She's been tied and screamin' for three days. I finally set Mary Jean to keep a hold of the little boys and not go near her momma. Even if he ain't Catholic, I fetched Preacher Haller."

Naomi understood. Preacher Haller had also been required to preach Aunt Wilma's funeral.

Mrs. Kruse got quieter and stretched out her fingers from her bound hand as if groping for someone's hand. Preacher Haller took her hand and motioned for Mr. Kruse to take the other. Instantly Sarah Mitchell laid her right hand over the comforting hands of Preacher Haller, and with her left hand began to caress Mrs. Kruse's head. Sarah crooned, "You'll be all right. You're going to make it, Mrs. Kruse. We're all here pulling for you. You're a strong woman. You're a strong woman." But Sarah Mitchell's eyes were misty.

Then Preacher Haller did a strange thing. He pulled Sarah Mitchell into the other room, as if it were she who needed the comfort now instead of Mrs. Kruse.

The phone rang.

Preacher Haller answered it and said, "Miss Mitchell, it's Faith Jackson. I mean Faith White. Forgive me, I forgit. Her time's come and she cain't git ahold of Dr. Foster. She wonders if you could make it over there right quick."

When they got to Faith White's, Faith and Chet were both in the kitchen. Faith was clutching one hand under her belly and the other to her back. She acted as if she hated to remove her hands, even to take *Pollyanna* when Naomi handed it to her.

Donny and Billy were carrying in stove wood, and Chet was trying to get a ham into the oven. Chet said, "I been savin' this ham till the day we got our baby. It's a glorious day, I'll tell y'that! Give me a hand here, Naomi, if y'will. It's takin' me forever to git this ham in. I'm as slow as a man with seven-year itch and six years behind on his scratchin'."

Just then Faith gave a sharp cry. "Chet, Chet, help me! I'm havin' it. Get me to the bed!"

Chet picked her up and carried her to a bed in the front room. Sarah followed as soon as she could say, "Naomi, keep the little boys out, and for heaven's sake, keep an eye on that ham, and on the beans too on top of the stove. Good grief!" But she was smiling as she left the room.

Faith was crying and yelling something awful, and the little boys began to cry too. Naomi wiped their noses. Billy blew real hard and said, "I got bad cold." Then he reached into the big Vicks jar on the kitchen cabinet and got a scoop of the salve on his finger and ate it.

"Billy Jackson, don't you doctor yourself. Y'ain't suppose to eat Vicks unless a grown-up gives it to you!"

"I'm Billy White. I turned White now, Naomi."

Little Donny ignored the talk and went right on crying. Naomi had to do something to keep the boys from being scared. Faith's cries scared even her. She took them out to the far woodpile out of hearing distance and got them to seeing who could throw wood chips the farthest. They stayed and played for a long time until a wild scream came from the house. Naomi looked back and saw smoke coming from the kitchen door.

"Stay out by this woodpile or I'll whip you good!" she told the boys. She ran to the kitchen. It was just the beans burning. She lifted the heavy iron kettle and quickly poured the unburned top portion of the pot of beans into a clean big stewer. Then she went out to the backyard to scrape out the burned part and to threaten the little boys again. She added more water to the stewer of beans and put it back on the stove. She hoped she was doing things right. Mom still wouldn't let her cook much, and she only did what seemed right, and it was awfully hard to think with Faith screaming and yelling.

Faith was crying, "I'm dyin'! Oh, Chet, honey, I'm dyin'." Naomi had never been near a woman in childbirth, but it was like Mom said; it was a woman's Fate to bear her children in pain. "Promise me, Chet, to take care of Billy and Donny. Don't let no one take them from you, Chet. Take good care of 'em. Oh, God, take me out of this pain and let me go with my momma. We're both goin', Chet. I love you, Chet." Then there was another great scream and, for a moment, silence. Then came the cry of a baby!

Laughter and weeping and shouting filled the house as Faith and Chet rejoiced. Sarah Mitchell came into the dining room carrying a crying baby girl, all red and wrinkled and with a creamy-white film covering its little naked body. It was the first time Naomi had ever seen a brand-new baby! She was so tiny, so perfect.

"Beautiful, isn't she?" Sarah asked as she laid a blanket on the table and put the baby on it and began to wipe her clean.

Naomi couldn't answer. Wasn't it something, a newborn

baby? Right here on this table was Faith and Chet's baby girl! Then she remembered Faith's cries. "Is Faith all right? She's not goin' to die?"

"Not at all. In fact, it was a beautiful delivery. Faith was scared and worried and let the world know it. But she's not worried now."

"But a woman's got to have pain," said Naomi. "Mom says it's Scripture."

"Most of Faith's pain would have gone if she hadn't been so scared. Someone needs to help a woman fight back her fears. I need more time to spend with people like Faith. Stop looking so concerned. Everything's just fine. Look at this beautiful little girl here!"

Just then Chet came through the dining-room door to claim his daughter. "Here, give me my little Hope! Ain't she a purty one, Naomi? Hey, I gotta show her to them boys. Where are the little rascals?"

Naomi went to the door to call the boys. She was ready to leave the happy White family by the time Sarah was. As she crawled back into Sarah's coupe she was smiling.

Sarah said, "Well now, that's more like your old self. Some occasion, huh? You like being a nurse, don't you? Is that why you wanted to be with me today? You been thinking about being a nurse? We could sure use some help."

"No, no, that ain't the reason I had to see you." Naomi felt a wave of fear as she remembered her own Fate again. They were on their way home, and it was tell Sarah either now or never. It had been good for a little while helping Sarah and not having time to think, but cancer didn't leave just by being ignored. The ugly word stuck and wouldn't come out. She started crying softly, and turned her head so that Sarah couldn't see.

But Sarah did see. She pulled to the side of the road and

stopped the car. "All right, Naomi, what is it? Has something happened at home? I swore I wouldn't interfere but—"

"No, it ain't Mom. It's me. I'm dyin' of cancer!"

At first Sarah's face was full of alarm, and then her expression settled back to her nurse's no-nonsense way. "What has happened to make you think this, Naomi?"

"I'm bleedin' jist like Mrs. Jackson. I've got the sign of cancer. It's jist like Mrs. . . ." Naomi stopped before saying the word "Jeno," for she had never told Sarah about Mrs. Jeno. She had somehow known that Sarah would be even worse than Dad when it came to not believing in fortunetellers.

Sarah looked relieved and began to smile. "Where are you bleeding? How—?"

Naomi didn't want to answer. She folded her hands and laid them protectively in her lap.

"Naomi Bradley, you've started your menses. Didn't your mom ever tell you—? No, I suppose she hasn't. . . . Look, Naomi, every woman must form extra blood just in case she'll get pregnant and needs it for the growth of the baby within her. Faith could never have had that beautiful little girl if she hadn't had her menses first. That's nature's way of providing for new life. And nature starts you practicing early."

"You mean it ain't—it ain't . . . ?" Naomi wasn't sure how to go on. It wasn't cancer for sure, or Sarah Mitchell wouldn't be looking so practical and certain, but along with relief Naomi was beginning to feel foolish.

"Just use a piece of cloth to catch that blood," said Sarah, "and be happy in knowing your body is healthy and working fine. Smile, Naomi! That blood is not the sign of death but the sign of new life coming some day. You're growing into a woman. Smile, Naomi!"

NINE

Naomi remembered the smile on Sarah Mitchell's face when Sarah had said, "I think you have a special talent for helping others, Naomi. You'd make a fine nurse. Not everyone is suited to a life of service, but you would be, Naomi. I know it."

Serve your fellowman. Love your neighbor. The Lord favored those who gave their life to service for others. Preachers gave service to others, but since that was out, maybe she would give some thought to being a nurse.

Still, Naomi wasn't sure she wanted to give her life over to service like Preacher Haller and Sarah Mitchell. She sort of would like to be married someday. Of course both Sarah and the preacher seemed perfectly happy, although they hadn't married. Preacher Haller had been just the picture of happiness, with a soft heavenly smile on his face, when he'd said last Sunday, "There ain't a problem in the world that cain't be licked by love and service. It's the second commandment. And on it hinges the answers to all our problems. Now I thank of my preachin' as bein' a service. Not just to the Lord but to my neighbor, too. And there's lots of other ways a body can be of service. Find a way to serve your fellowman, and you'll find a way to please the

Lord. Nothin' could make the Lord happier than seein' us all findin' lives of service."

Naomi stayed after church to talk to him a little more about service. She'd felt especially close to Preacher Haller ever since she'd heard him pray for Mrs. Kruse, who was a Catholic. It had made Naomi feel good. For a long time she had suspected that, if God loved everyone, that had to include Catholics, too. Now Preacher Haller had proved it.

When Preacher Haller saw her waiting, he smiled and mussed her hair. "Well, Naomi, you got any big worries today, like, say, about cookin', or when you're goin' to marry, or somethin'?"

Naomi kept her own smile. "No, I ain't worried about either one."

"That's fine, that's fine," said Preacher Haller. "Take no thought for the morrow, the Lord says."

He was teasing. She thought she'd give him a little back. "You ever worry about gettin' married?"

Preacher Haller seemed to enjoy nothing more than a good game of teasing. "Why, Paul the Apostle was a good man, and he didn't have a wife."

"Jist like Sarah Mitchell. She's a good woman, and she don't have no husband."

Naomi was proud she'd thought up her own snappy counterexample so fast, but the game was over already. Preacher Haller suddenly remembered he'd forgotten to pick up the hymnbooks. He hadn't even given her a chance to get serious. She'd wanted to discuss service with him. Her fourteenth birthday wasn't so many months off, and she wanted to continue to feel as happy as she did now. She still carried a good feeling about helping Sarah Mitchell on her rounds.

It had made her feel good, too, to know that Mrs. Jackson had felt a little hopeful before she died. When she saw the baby, Mrs. Jackson had said, "I'm ready, Lord. You can call me home now." And she died that very night. Everyone said she was such a hard worker that she was sure to be numbered among the saints. Naomi was glad she had been of service to Mrs. Jackson.

"Speakin' of service, Naomi," Paul said after the sermon at church, "how'd you like to be of service to me and do the barn chores?" Paul was too young, but he wanted time to go out on dates during harvest season, when money was plentiful, like Pete and Jay and Ike. Helping him was hardly what Preacher Haller meant by service.

Harvest was a fine time of year for everyone. Folks on the radio said a big war was going on over in Europe and that America ought to prepare in case she was to get into it. There was even talk of a draft—men having to go into the Army whether they wanted to or not. But even if all that was true, it didn't affect people in these parts much. If the country was to go to war, southeast Missouri was so far from the big cities that an enemy would never find it.

Mom was busy making pumpkin pies. Grace was learning to sew and was making skirts for the school year ahead. Naomi gathered in the sweet potatoes, which weighed at least a pound apiece, and scrubbed them and put them in the oven to bake brown in their jackets. Bruce and Benny were making kites out of the *Kansas City Star* to fly in the gusts of wind that were already pulling leaves from the trees.

Preacher Haller said, "Harvest bein' brought in makes the religious feelin's of thanksgiving hit a peak. I'm callin' a revival."

The men of the community got together to build a brush arbor of a large size, because no church could hold the expected congregation. The first night everyone in the whole country came. Mom saw to it that everybody in the Bradley family attended, too.

What came unexpected was a message from Sarah Mitchell that she'd like Naomi to pick her up the night of the revival. She needed help to get someone to the meeting.

Neither Mom nor Dad forbade Naomi to go. No one could forbid another to come out to a revival. Not even the worst of sinners could be forbidden, for one never knew when they might get converted. It was not only a service, it was also Naomi's Christian duty to see to it that Sarah Mitchell and whoever else she had coming got to the revival. Naomi could hardly wait to find out who the other person was.

Mrs. Kruse? A Catholic was coming to a revival? Sarah Mitchell explained in the car on the way to Kruses'. "She feels she has to come, as a way to show respect and to give thanks to Preacher Haller for his help when she was sick. She's still weak, and I don't think she needs this emotional strain, but she'll have it no other way. I just need you to come along with us. You don't mind, do you, Naomi? I'm not real sure I remember how to act in church myself." Sarah looked down for a minute. "And I'm not sure that the people will welcome either me or Mrs. Kruse."

Naomi couldn't say no to Sarah or to Mrs. Kruse.

When they arrived at the Kruses' house, Mary Jean was waiting too. She was puffing as she slid into the car next to Naomi and whispered, "I've always wondered what went on at revival meetings. It won't be a sin for me to go. I'm jist going along with Mother to say thanks to a man who came to help when he was needed. I'm not really going to church."

It was too dark for anyone to see them as they got out of the car at the brush arbor. They walked in quietly and sat down in the back row.

Naomi's brothers, including Paul, sat on the benches just outside the arbor out of the lanterns' light so they could hold hands with their girls. Bruce and Benny chased other little boys in the darkened woods just past the range of Mom and Dad's shouts.

Little girls didn't join in the chase. They sat dutifully on benches and listened to the message of Preacher Haller. It would be up to them to see that the souls of their future children were saved. Mom had always seen to it that both Naomi and Grace sat still, even when they were tiny. But Mom couldn't force Grace to listen.

Chet and Faith White came in with their three children. Chet was so proud. He marched right up to the front bench and sat down next to the tree that the bench was nailed to, and rubbed his back against it in comfort. Chet never let anybody bother him in his happiness. When Mr. Walker made reference to the fact that it was great now that he had his very own kid to raise, Chet quickly told him, "Listen here, if I had you take off your clothes and run through a briar patch, could you come out and tell me which briar went deepest? How do you know these babies ain't all mine?" Folks said no more.

Great waves of song filled the arbor just as Mrs. Jeno and her children came in. But every man, woman, and child forgot their differences and continued to sing praises to the Lord God Almighty.

Then the sacrament was passed. A large glass of wine was passed along for each person to take a sip, and when it was Mrs. Brown's retarded boy's turn he drank it all.

People grew quiet, little girls tittered, laughs cracked the silence. Sarah Mitchell leaned toward Naomi and whispered, "Isn't it sad? Why don't people go on without a fuss? The boy can't be expected to know. Why don't they look at themselves? The adults here should know that germs are passed from mouth to mouth with that glass, anyway."

Someone overheard her and whispered authoritatively, "It's sacrament wine, there's no danger."

Naomi thought for a moment that Sarah Mitchell had been guilty of judging, but said nothing. Preacher Haller had begun his sermon.

"My topic tonight is forgivin' the sinner. Let a body who's bogged down in ways of evil, let any person who's yielded to his weaknesses find hope in his fellowman's ability to forgive him as well as in God's great forgiveness." Each phrase got louder than the one before. It was a good opening. "Let us all follow the ways of the Master and forget the evil past of our brothers and sisters and welcome them into a new world filled with hope and forgiveness. Let us look on the convert as a new person delivered of the influences of the devil. Let them stand whole and pure in our minds!"

"Hallelujah! Thank the Lord!" cried Mrs. Brown.

Mrs. Kruse was restless in her seat; then she stood up and in an unnatural way said, "Hallelujah! Thank the Lord." It was exactly the right thing to do. Mrs. Kruse reached out as if to embrace all the sisters sitting near her. The question now was, would the sisters answer to her love?

"Hallelujah!" echoed several other voices, and Naomi relaxed.

"Hallelujah," shouted Preacher Haller. "This good Sister Kruse has been delivered from the hands of Satan and from the bounds that had her tied tighter than any rope ever could. She is well and whole and stands before us a changed woman. Let us all rejoice in her deliverance. Let us all rejoice in her new strength and her new life. From now on she's a free woman—free to live the laws of God and find happiness. Who among us could find fault with her? Who among us might not have weakened and fallen by the wayside of morphine addiction if the circumstances had been like unto hers?"

Someone whispered, "I thought it was Catholicism she was giving up, not morphine." Little groups of whispers started to rise around the arbor. Sarah Mitchell tensed, and Mrs. Kruse held tight to Mary Jean's hand and looked scared.

146

Before Naomi, or anyone for that matter, had time to know what to do, Mrs. Jeno had walked up to the front of the arbor meeting. She looked beautiful in her lovely blue dress, and she drew every bit as much attention as Naomi had once dreamed of doing as a powerful woman preacher.

"Listen to me," she said. "There ain't no use for us to backbite Mrs. Kruse. In the city where me and my husband lived there was lots of churches, a good many of them Catholic churches. I lived right across the street from a Catholic, and she never done me any harm. You all might as well git use to the idea of havin' a Catholic church near you too, because in less than a year you'll see one right here in your midst, and a priest at the head of it too. Mrs. Kruse can call on her own kind in time of need and won't have to be beholden."

Mom got up and started to leave. A couple of other women arose, and then a man, and then Grace. Soon everyone, just about, was standing up.

Preacher Haller's voice came loud above their talk. "All right, now. Ever'body set down. Hear me, set down!"

People obeyed. It came natural to obey a preacher.

"Now this is my church. This is my job, to preach a sermon, and that's what I've come to do and that's what I'm gonna do. I'll thank Mrs. Jeno and Mrs. Kruse for their good intentions. I'll leave it up to ever' one of you to believe what he wonts. Jesus never forced no one to believe. That wasn't His job, and I don't take it to be mine. Mine is to preach a revival and now that y're all back in your seats, I'll jist git on with it!

Brothers and sisters, it's born in all of us to test and try the Lord as we are learnin' life's ways. Like a baby who's learnin' to walk and falls, do we shout him down agin because he wasn't perfect?" Preacher Haller's voice was loud and beautifully rhythmic, and his hands beat the pulpit with great thunder. " 'Course we don't. We give him a

147

hand and a smile and a little help to stand alone. We forgit his fall. Let us forgit the falls of our adult members of this society for they, too, are but babes in the eyes of the Lord, babes tryin' to find the right way to walk. And the Lord don't forgive begrudgingly. Let's not be guilty of makin' God in our image. Let's try to make our ways in the image of our Lord. To Him a sin is a sin. Little or big, He forgives *all* sins. Let us have it in our hearts to forgive all sins of *all* people! This world wouldn't be in a war now if all people lived the laws of forgiveness and love. Amen!"

Sarah Mitchell was getting up and leaving. Naomi could see that Mrs. Kruse didn't hardly know if she should follow or stay seated. The meeting wasn't about to be over! There was still to be lots of singing and the call to repentance and more, so why was she leaving?

Naomi was about to run and catch Sarah and explain all this to her when a loud voice shouted, "Stop! Stop, Sister Mitchell!"

Preacher Haller was back in the pulpit again and waving desperately. "Listen, ever'one. I'm the blackest sinner of all. I stand to hear my own words. I've borne a heart burned black with five long years of unforgiveness. I've failed to see this woman, Sarah Mitchell, standing pure and whole before me. Will you forgive me, Sister Mitchell?" His voice rose higher and higher. "Forgive my unforgiveness! Will you marry me, Sarah? Will you marry me?" The last sentence came out as a grand and glorious pleading shout.

A tremendous gasp went up from the congregation, and everyone sat still. Even the younger boys, running out in back, came in close to listen.

"Yes, I'll marry you, Jim Haller. Yes, I will." And the same tenderness and the same gentle tears Naomi had witnessed when Sarah Mitchell held the brow of Mrs. Kruse were there again. But now Sarah also smiled, a wonderful wide smile, and her eyes shone with love and longing. She looked like an angel standing there in a halo of yellow lantern light.

It was evident to anyone who cared to look at her that Sarah Mitchell felt she had gotten the best of rewards from the good Lord for her years of service. As close as Naomi had been to her, she had never guessed that Sarah sought to be friends with anyone else, that she had wanted to *marry* Preacher Jim Haller! Naomi supposed *she* ought to be happy too, for she'd obviously done Preacher Haller and Sarah a good service by getting Sarah here tonight. There they were, both of them, all smiles.

After the meeting everyone had whispered that what Preacher Haller had chosen to forgive Sarah Mitchell was her having had a baby and put it out for adoption. Naomi still didn't want to believe that, and she longed to ask Sarah about it point-blank. If she did, it'd mean for sure she'd lose Sarah as a friend, but she was losing her anyway, wasn't she?

The next morning after breakfast she walked over to Sarah's. As she passed by the cleared flower bed in front of the house, she noticed that Sarah had even cut down the dead flowers after the frost had hit them. She was the neatest woman! But certainly no woman to pattern after.

Sarah's face was still glowing as she invited Naomi in for a cup of cocoa, but the first chance she got, Naomi asked anyway, "Did you really have a baby and give it away?"

Sarah didn't act too hurt or surprised but answered simply, "No."

"Ever'body thanks that's what Preacher Haller forgive you of."

"I know, Naomi. And that is exactly what Jim thought he forgave me of." Sarah smiled again.

"You didn't do it, and you let him believe you did? All these years, you let him believe . . ." What a thing for Sarah to do! What a waste! What a waste!

"I didn't *let* Jim believe it," said Sarah. "He chose to listen to gossip."

"How could you let him go on believin' it if you loved him? Y'must've loved him. Y'sure loved him when he proposed."

"Yes, I sure did." Sarah got that same radiant look on her face again. "Jim Haller had just grown into the man I'd hoped he would—into the man I'd want to marry, a man who would be capable of forgiving a loved one for making an error."

"But y'didn't. There was no use of y'bein' an old maid and havin' people talk bad about you an'—"

"And good about me. Don't you hear good talk too, Naomi? It was worth the wait. I hope that one day you'll understand it was worth the wait. Are you all set for the wedding, Naomi?"

There wasn't any sense wasting more time with Sarah talking in circles. She'd go home and think about it.

But Naomi hardly had time to think at home these days with all the wedding announcements she was hearing. Even Ike had got himself engaged.

The next time she saw Sarah, Naomi said, "Ever'body's tryin' to figure whether it was Preacher Haller proposin' to you or Pearl Harbor that's made a streak on marryin'."

"Well, I don't think either is a valid excuse to rush into a marriage." Sarah sounded serious, and Naomi had meant her statement to sound a little funny, just to show she was friendly again. There wasn't any use in discussing certain things with certain people.

Now Mom had been tickled to death about all the marrying. She and Grace had been discussing about every boy in the country, trying to figure out who'd be a good beau for Grace. Grace was fourteen already and old enough to be considering.

That had really made Paul mad. He was sixteen, and Dad still felt he wasn't really old enough to date. But Mom said girls grew up faster than boys, and she was right about that. Everyone kept noticing that Naomi's body had grown to womanhood, but no one said a word about Paul looking like a man.

Anyway, Sarah wasn't one to discuss such matters with now. "I got to be goin'," Naomi told her. "We got a few bolls left in the cotton patch, and I plan to pull some today. It don't hardly pay enough to go to the field after them, but a penny's a penny."

As Naomi started out the door, Sarah reminded her that the wedding was only two weeks away. Then she laughed. "Are you planning a new dress for my special day?"

Naomi smiled and nodded her head, and went to join Paul in the cottonfield, where he was pulling bolls with a fury.

"Dad says I gotta take you and Grace with me to see *The Cisco Kid* movie tonight. Darlene is gonna love that! Other guys are lined up jist waitin' for me to blow it with Darlene, and Dad has to—"

Pete put in, "You might as well forgit Darlene. Jay says they're making Malden into a Army air base. Some of the soldiers are already movin' in. Jay says he'd better git married like Ike, or be sole support on the farm, or somethin', before the draft gits him. Jay says he ain't inlistin'. He ain't leavin' his gal to no Army air base full of soldiers."

A fear surged through Naomi, a fear she had been pushing back continually since she was eleven. Air base? If there was to be an air base, then . . . "Will they be bringing in planes?" she asked quietly.

151

"Already startin' to," said Pete. "Didn't you see that bunch come in this mornin'? Where was you this mornin'? Good gosh, they made plenty of racket. I hear they're flyin' in men and supplies. It won't be long before the sky right here will be swarmin' with planes." Pete finished the sentence by sweeping his arms high and wide.

"Oh, no, jist like Mrs. Jeno said!" Pete had used her exact words.

Paul stopped his boll pulling. "That's right! That damn fortune-teller did say that, didn't she? Now look here, Naomi, don't start gettin' dramatic on us. You ain't gonna die. So she lucked out a couple of times! Is that enough to git worked up over?"

Naomi couldn't say a word. Fear had its claws in her voice box.

Paul said, "And don't you start none of that sad talk of yours tonight at the movie. If you mention one word about that fortune-teller, I'll . . ."

Paul needn't worry, she wouldn't mention it. She wouldn't let herself get worked up about it anymore. She had done everything she could think of to have God add to her years. She would not worry. She was going to live the same as Grace, and she was going to get married like Grace and have pretty little babies and do all the things women do in life. She heard Mom praying every night for her and Grace's souls, praying that they'd turn out good women. Mom knew Mrs. Jeno's spell was off. Why else would she have mentioned Naomi's name, too, in her prayers?

By the time she and Grace went to the movie with Paul and Darlene, Naomi had worked herself into a cheerful mood. Listening to the soft foreign accent of the Cisco Kid helped that mood grow, but after it was over, Paul suddenly began pulling her and Grace through the lobby and out the door.

Grace said, "Paul, quit jerkin' me. I'm gonna tell Dad how you're actin'. Where's Darlene?"

Paul glanced back toward the popcorn machine, and there was Darlene, smiling up prettily at a boy named Quick Silver and stealing a bite of his popcorn. Quick Silver wasn't his real name. His real name was Sylvester Q. Jenkins. His dad owned the farm-implement store, and Quick Silver owned a chrome-plated Harley Davidson motorcycle!

He was the only really handsome boy Naomi had ever seen. She stopped to have a look at him, and Quick Silver quipped, "I got your number, baby!" just as Paul jerked her the rest of the way out the door.

"Paul, you cain't leave Darlene. Her dad said for you to make sure you got her home safe and sound."

"Who the hell says I cain't leave her? No woman is triflin' with my affections!"

Paul started down the street, but he hadn't gotten three stores away when he stopped. A soldier was talking to Pete. Paul stopped to listen in, and Naomi and Grace had no choice but to stop and listen too.

The soldier was a young boy of about eighteen, the same age as Jay. He had deep brown-red hair and would have been nice-enough looking except for a mass of pimples on his face. He was telling about the day they took him into the Army.

"Boy, they had us walkin' around in our birthday suits for fourteen hours." He noticed Grace and Naomi, paused for only a second, and added, "It was already turnin' cold, but that's the Army for you."

Grace said, "Didn't y'git to eat for fourteen hours?"

"Oh, sure, they let us eat. We went down to this one big room that was jist brimful of barrels of sauerkraut and wieners, and we got to take all we wanted. But I'm tellin' you, I always did have a sensitive stomach. Born that way, I guess."

153

Pete said, "This is Lenis McMannen, and he's from a farm in Kansas. His friends call him Lenny."

Paul seemed to have forgotten Darlene completely, and he set right in to a good conversation with Lenny until he finally remembered what Dad had told him. "Look, Lenny, why don't you walk for a little way with us? I wont to hear more about the Army, but I got to start home with my sisters now."

Lenny seemed glad to walk along. He and Paul kept talking, with Pete and Grace saying a word now and then. Naomi never talked, for she didn't know what to say to a soldier. She lagged behind the others.

Finally Paul said, "Heck, Lenny, I ain't finished talkin' yet. But if you're gonna walk all the way home with us, y'might as well stay the night, if Uncle Sam'll let you."

"I don't know. I don't have to be back till tomorrow. You sure it won't be puttin' you out?"

Grace and Paul and even Pete assured him it would be fine. Naomi wasn't sure that Mom would agree. Mom never took to anyone staying overnight.

Paul was right about Lenny being welcome. Mom fluttered around in a most unnatural way to make Lenny feel really welcome. When it came time for breakfast the next day, she fixed fried eggs and even got a piece of fresh pork Dad had just butchered and made a special milk gravy with it. Then she went in the front room and asked Lenny, "What do you folks usually eat for breakfast in Kansas?"

"Oh, anything'll do for me. Don't make any fuss at all. Jist a little bit of cracked wheat'll be fine. That's what we usually eat at home."

Mom came back into the kitchen huffing, her face full of movement as she tried to talk and think and manage. "If we only had— We do! Naomi, git that box of wheat stuff off the top shelf. Now I know why I saved it all this time. Git it down and git it made. Git a move on!"

Naomi had been the one who had asked Dad to buy that box of Wheatena two years ago. She had made half the box then, and no one had liked it, but Mom had been too saving to throw it out. Now Naomi reread the directions and cooked the wheat mush. She could hear Grace at the dining-room table explaining to Lenny how Pete had gotten rid of his pimples by using a mixture of raw egg and buttermilk. The conversation went on until Naomi came in with the bowl of mush.

Mom said, "Here's your cracked wheat. Now you go right at it. Let me scoop y'some out in a saucer. Glad we had it on hand. None of my family cares for it, but if that's what you like, you go right ahead and eat all you wont."

Grace said, "I like it. I'll jist have me a saucerful too, if y'don't mind." Grace took the last from the bowl except for a scrape or two.

Mom handed Naomi the bowl and said, "Here, take this back to the kitchen. It's empty."

On the way back to the kitchen Naomi thought she'd take a bite. It was hard to remember how a thing tasted such a long time ago. She scraped up the remains with the serving spoon and almost had it to her mouth when she saw that some of those little hard brown spots weren't wheat bran at all, but bugs! It was full of little cooked bugs. Mom ought to have known that flour is nothing but wheat, and if flour can't set too long, for fear of bugs, then cracked wheat would be the same! Naomi couldn't tell them. If Mom found out, she'd kill her.

She went back to the table and took a fried egg off the platter. There were two left, but she didn't feel that hungry. She watched Grace and Lenny eating mouthful after mouthful of buggy wheat and talking and enjoying themselves while doing it.

Lenny said, "This is real good, Naomi. You're a good cook."

Grace said, "She cain't cook at all. This is the first thing she's cooked since I can remember. I do 'most all the cookin'."

Lenny smiled at Naomi anyway and said, "It's delicious, Naomi."

Naomi couldn't swallow the egg in her mouth but ran to the back porch, found the slop bucket, and vomited.

She came back in when breakfast was over. Lenny was saying good-bye, and when he noticed Naomi, he looked very sympathetic. "I know how it is to have a weak stomach, Naomi. I've had one all my life, born that way, I reckon. Well, I'll see you folks around town next week, I reckon."

When he left, Grace said, "You stay away from Lenny, hear?" Naomi saw it right off. Grace wanted Lenny for a beau. Imagine having a beau who ate bugs! Yech!

Grace acted as if Lenny had been talking just to her, even though he'd said what he said to the whole family.

After that Grace filled each day with her anxiety about seeing Lenny again until it was a relief to have the weekend come and to get her into Malden. Grace wore her new dress, which she had ordered from Sears for the weddings, so Naomi wore hers too. Grace had a blue dress to match her eyes; Naomi's was white rayon taffeta with ruffles at the hem and sleeves. It had cost one dollar and had to be washed by hand, the directions said. But then all clothes got washed by hand at the Bradleys', so that was just fine.

The first thing Naomi noticed in town was some soldiers sitting out in front of Mr. Bell's grocery store. They were all drinking pop. One of them was Lenny, and he got up to meet them. "Hi, Naomi. Hi, Grace. I got one of my buddies here if you want to meet him. Come here, Grace, I want you to meet Rob———"

"Naomi and me don't wont to meet anybody else. Naomi's not old enough yet. She's jist thirteen. I'm older."

156

"Well . . ." Lenny was smiling, and hardly knew what to say. Naomi didn't want to meet the other soldier, just like Grace had said. She didn't want to talk to Lenny either. Grace had her eye on him, and he ought to know it.

Lenny was still fumbling for something to say. "Well, there ain't nothin' wrong in bein' thirteen, I guess."

Grace was forcing a smile through set lips. "There is, too, if you're goin' to die before you're fourteen! It's true. The fortune-teller told her."

Lenny set his bottle of pop down. Naomi was afraid his sensitive stomach was about to act up.

Grace said, "Where'd y'git the pop? I thank I could use a bottle." She took Lenny's hand and they walked into the store.

Lenny made sure to keep a wide distance as they walked past Naomi. He acted as if she were a ghost already. She felt like yelling "Boo" right in his face. Some soldier he was going to make!

In the week before the Haller-Mitchell wedding, Grace spent most of her time figuring how to duck away with Lenny. Or she was busy figuring out a way to get Paul to invite Lenny out to spend the night again. Paul wasn't too hard to persuade. He liked Lenny.

Lenny was there for supper again Saturday night, and Grace told Naomi, "Stay out of the kitchen! I'm cookin'."

So Naomi set the table and carried in the milk from the pumphouse. Paul and Lenny were in the barn looking at the horses, and it was a good thing, as it turned out. A hurt cry rang out from the kitchen. Naomi ran in to see Mom scraping ruffled frosting off the edge of a fluffy white cake. Grace was crying and clutching her arm, where the prints of Mom's fingers still showed.

Mom was screaming, "Don't start it, Grace! Don't start it! He's a good boy and 'll make a fine husband, but men

157

don't take to all this finery. Wilma'll be the death of me yet! It never got her a man, Grace, and it won't help you none, neither. Now dry up and smooth out this cake. Let him go by the taste. Frills will work against you, not for you. Mark my word."

Naomi quickly backed back into the dining room. She felt strange. It was as if she had *had* to witness this scene. It was as if she had to know, at long last, that it was Aunt Wilma Mom hated, and not just her. It was Grace this time who had tried Aunt Wilma's ways.

But was it Aunt Wilma after all? Or was Mom just afraid that Grace wouldn't get her man? Naomi figured Grace would get Lenny, and Mom shouldn't worry. How was it Sarah Mitchell could sit around for five years and think it was worth it, and Mom couldn't allow Grace to make one mistake, to miss one chance? If Mom knew that Quick Silver had flirted with Naomi, she'd start pushing that too. Yet Sarah Mitchell had gotten her man, or would tomorrow if the wedding came off without a hitch.

Of course nothing could possibly go wrong at a preacher's wedding. God wouldn't allow it. Oh, Mom and a few other people did mention that there might be some problems between them with Sarah promising Dr. Foster to keep at her nursing. Dr. Foster insisted it was Sarah's Christian duty not to walk out when she was so sorely needed, and Preacher Haller seemed to agree.

As Dad said, "He's not buyin' a pig in a poke. He knowed she was a nurse. He could've backed out anytime if he'da wanted to. Now he's made his bed, let him sleep in it." Everybody laughed, and that was the general feeling all around.

A preacher came all the way from Sikeston to perform the wedding, and that night Naomi put a little slice of the wedding cake under her pillow, so she'd happily dream of her own future husband.

It didn't work at all! Instead of a nice dream, she had this awful nightmare where a bunch of soldiers were riding silver Harleys through a burning jungle trying to catch a beautiful lioness. Boy, was it good to wake up and find that it was only a dream. Such rushing! The poor lioness had had no time to choose which direction she would take.

Naomi knew one thing for sure. She'd be the choosiest woman in the world, maybe wait longer than Sarah Mitchell. Why, she'd wait ten years for a *good* man, and she might even be a woman of service as well as a married one. Gosh was that ever a silly dream!

TEN

The planes from Malden Air Base swooped low to scare old Turner and Jill as they plowed the field. Naomi watched as the planes dropped bags of flour on Mr. Jackson's barn when the pilots missed their target marked X. They were playacting.

Good common sense told Naomi that there really was a war, or else there wouldn't be soldiers and planes swarming just about everywhere, but the planes dropped flour bombs and the soldiers smiled. Maybe that was the best way to handle disaster: get ready just in case and then smile. Like Mom putting up plenty of food against the winter, and extra in case of floods or a poor year, then forgetting the oncoming shortage.

Dad had told Naomi a long time ago to forget Mrs. Jeno's words. He should have explained that it helps to pretend that nothing's going to happen anyway. Naomi's birthday was creeping closer daily, but she'd managed to get her mind on other things through this method. First, she never missed a day of church; second, she helped others often, like God wanted her to do; third, she let faith make her say, "I ain't dyin' before I'm fourteen"; and fourth, she smiled.

Naomi wasn't the only one around the house who smiled. Grace had been smiling her head off for over two months now, and Mom was about as bad. Mom had gotten her wish and Grace had married Lenny. Grace was fourteen, drawing near to fifteen, when they had the wedding. Dad took them all in the pickup to Arkansas because Missouri law said Grace had to be fifteen. Grace said it didn't matter how young she was now. In twenty years who'd ask questions anyway?

At one point in the getting-ready part of the wedding, Mom had gotten mad at Naomi and, along with her other shouting, had said, "See, looks don't count. A man looks for a woman who can manage. Grace got her man, didn't she? And her not much older than Wilma when she come to mooch off us."

But looks did count. Grace had started looking beautiful as soon as she knew that Lenny had eyes just for her. Grace still looked kind of pretty in the face and eyes. It was funny that Mom didn't see it too. Once again Naomi wondered if Mom had ever been pretty.

Grace now got an allotment check from the Army, so she paid Mom room and board. Lenny got to come home to the farm on weekends. Lenny was not good-looking, but he was nice. Maybe looks didn't count with Grace. Naomi wanted someone good-looking *and* nice, like Preacher Haller was.

Naomi wanted to get Mom on the subject of the allotment check, because she had a mighty big thing to ask of Mom, and she needed her in the right frame of mind. She waited until after school on a snowy soft day. Then she waited for the perfect moment—after the noon chores were over and before Mom had started her supper chores—to ask her lead-up question.

Mary Jean Kruse had been hired by the dime store in Malden, and surely Naomi could do a job like that too.

She had to get Mom to agree. "Mom, what you plannin' to buy with Grace's room-and-board money?"

"I don't know that that's any of your business, but I don't mind tellin' you. I'm hopin', and your Dad is hopin' too, that with enough scrimpin' and savin' we can git electricity brung in. That's one good wind that's blowed in with all this air base comin'. The power lines is close enough now, we're considerin'.' "

So that was Mom's dream. Preacher Haller and Sarah had electricity already, and it sure made a bright light. A little extra money would help Mom get her electricity, too.

"Mom, I've been workin' up to ask if I could go with Mary Jean Kruse tomorrer and see if I could hire on at the dime store and work on Saturdays. Mary Jean says they need extra help Saturdays. I could pay room and board just like Grace."

A shine hit Mom's face immediately, before she had a chance to darken it with studied seriousness. Naomi let Mom take her time about answering, for she was sure now of a yes. Mom said, "It would be a better help than y'are around here in the wintertime. How y'plan on gettin' into town?"

"I can git a ride in with Mary Jean. Mr. Kruse takes her. I could wait at the end of the lane, and he'd give me a ride into town. Mary Jean wonts me to stay all night with her tonight, for the first time, so's she can tell me jist who I got to see and what to say. Can I do it, Mom? I jist got to git hired on at the dime store." Really she and Mary Jean needed to plan what to do about telling the manager that Naomi wasn't quite as old as Mary Jean.

"I didn't say y'couldn't, did I? Go on. Y'better be gittin' a move on if y're plannin' on goin' over to the Kruses' before dark. Mrs. Kruse don't talk none to you about bein' Catholic, does she?"

"No, she don't do that, Mom. I jist talk to Mary Jean mostly."

"And when y'start workin' in that dime store and start talkin' to any of them soldiers that come in, y'll have to watch your step there too, for I hear there's a good many Catholics among 'em. We ain't lettin' y' marry no Catholic."

"Mom, I ain't gettin' married for a long time. I ain't gonna talk to no soldiers!"

"There's some good ones among them. Grace couldn't ask for a better man than Lenny is. Y'll soon turn fourteen. Y'll be graduatin' from the eighth grade in May. Y're old enough to be considerin'. But we ain't lettin' you marry no Catholic. So that better be the first thing you find out. And y'ain't gonna date nobody. They can come out to the house like Lenny did."

There wasn't any use in talking further with Mom on that subject. She needed to be thinking about what clothes to wear when she went job hunting. She had only one pretty thing, a purple corduroy skirt. If only she had something to go with it. Mary Jean Kruse wore a turtleneck sweater with her skirt.

Naomi ran out the back door in search of Paul. Paul was in the barn wrapping a rope around his arm from his elbow to his hand and back again. "Can I talk to you, Paul?"

"I don't know, can you?"

"Paul, you know what I mean."

"Okay, Naomi, what's it this time? I'm worn out. I just took the twins for a ride on that sled Ike made. I oughta've made a new one. Them boys are gettin' too big to pull. I say if they're big enough to walk into town to school and stay with us year round, then they're big enough to pull each other."

Paul didn't look half as mad as he sounded, and Benny and Bruce were still out playing in the snow. They'd better make the most of it. Snow never lasted. "Paul, can I wear your turtleneck sweater to go in to see if I can git a job at the dime store on Saturdays like Mary Jean Kruse? Mom wants me to go to work so's I can pay board like Grace."

"Naomi, y'ain't in no court. You don't have to give me the whole case. No, y'cain't wear my sweater."

"Okay. I ain't goin' to crease your jeans no more for you to wear on Saturday nights." Naomi turned to walk back into the house, but she knew Paul would stop her.

"All right. That's blackmail, and if y'dare tell a soul that it's my sweater you're wearin', I'll—"

"I won't tell nobody, Paul, for I don't want them to know it myself." What bothered Paul most, of course, was that the sweater would fit both him and Naomi. Being small as a boy can be pitiful.

She got herself all dressed, put her coat on, and was fixing to leave when Grace said, "I thank it might be a good idea if you pushed the collar of Paul's sweater down so's Paul or Mom don't see it." Grace had stopped tattling so much now that she was married.

"Paul let me borrow it. He knows I'm wearin' it. If I'da known it had that orange pop spilled on it I might not've asked the favor." Naomi opened her coat to show Grace the spot.

Grace said, "Oh, no one will notice. What's a orange spot on a orange tweed sweater? Close your coat. Mom's comin'."

It was too late, Mom was there. "Naomi, take Paul's sweater off right this minute. You know what the Scriptures say about women that wear men's clothin'!"

"Mom, Paul said I could wear it, and Mary Jean Kruse has one jist like it, only in another color. She bought hers from the woman's counter at the store. So it ain't really a man's or a woman's. I mean, it can be either one. I gotta wear it. I need it."

"All right, go on if you wont, but mark my word, don't

ever expect the Lord to show you an ounce of mercy if you go contrary to His word." Naomi walked to the mirror to straighten the collar. Mom said, "No one makes their own looks, Naomi, so no use smilin' at that mirror. You got no right to collect flowers on the looks God give you. God'll show you no mercy."

So Naomi left with Mom's warnings ringing clear and loud in her ears. But God knew that this was an either-or. She wished Mom wouldn't talk like that about looks. She'd be glad to get to the Kruses. Mrs. Kruse was always so nice. Maybe Mary Jean would be making a cake for supper.

When she got there, she asked Mary Jean if they couldn't make a chocolate cake. That was Naomi's favorite. Mary Jean shook her head and answered, "No. Cain't make a cake tonight. Mama don't let me do things like that anymore, except on special occasions. In some ways she's worse than when she was on morphine." Mary Jean cupped her hand over her mouth and then, after a moment of looking scared, took it down and said, "I didn't mean to say that. I'm so glad Mama is well. I never want her sick like that again. It's jist . . . she's stricter. I don't want to talk about it. 'Sides, Dolly Russel wants us to come keep her company. She's watching the apartment for Reela while she's gone. I asked Daddy to take us over. It's all right with you, ain't it? We can make a cake or do anything we want over there. Reela is gone to St. Louis for a week. Dolly told me to bring you along when she found out I'd asked you to stay over at my house."

Naomi hadn't expected this turn of events. She'd sure like to see Reela's fancy apartment, which she'd gotten after marrying a city fellow. "Mom jist said . . . Well, I'm lucky jist to git to come over to your house . . . But . . . Reela and Dolly are almost relatives, what with Abe bein' married to their sister Mabel. Why, Reela and Dolly are almost my sisters-in-law by marriage."

"Oh, good. Daddy, we're ready if you'll drive us into Malden."

Mr. Kruse was there in a flash, and before Naomi could finish thinking things out, she was obeying a grown-up and getting into the front seat of Mr. Kruse's pickup. It was too late to admit to herself that neither Mom nor Dad thought too highly of Reela. Reela had a beautiful apartment above the dime store in Malden. People said she'd even had special painters out from Poplar Bluff to fix the place up. Reela said that she was going to live in Malden close to her mother until her husband got back from service overseas. But Abe said her husband was no soldier; he was in prison for embezzlement and Reela was waiting until his time was up.

Mom had said, "Reela was bound to turn out like her father. When it's in the blood, it'll come out. It's pure luck neither Mabel nor Dolly took after their father. Reela is his spittin' image, as much as a girl can be. Folks all know that some of the Russel money that they spent on their pretty clothes was from crooked dealin' Mr. Russel did on the side. Not all of it come from his workin' on the railroad, but who could prove it, with him bein' gone most all the time? But blood will out."

Naomi tried to make her thoughts go on to other things. She couldn't ask Mr. Kruse to turn around and go back.

Things sure looked different near Malden. Where fields had once stood there were now barracks and airplanes and other Army stuff. Gosh, there was sure lots of it. People said that the government had chosen Malden because it was hidden out of sight of the enemy, but as big as this air base was growing, anyone, friend or enemy, couldn't help but see it.

The town was changing too. There had never been a pinup picture of a movie star in the hardware-store window before. Not in Naomi's whole memory had there been one.

When Mr. Kruse stopped the truck and let them out, Naomi followed Mary Jean up the stairway that led to Reela's apartment. Even the stairway was beautiful. The wallpaper had a background that shone like gold. Walking into the apartment was like walking into a world of the movies. It even smelled like the movies.

"Gosh, I thought you girls would never git here. I popped you some corn while I was waitin'." Dolly Russel was as little and as pretty as the Christmas doll she was named for. She looked right at home among the fancy stuffed furniture and wooden tables that shone so you'd've thought it were wet varnish.

Naomi was glad she'd worn her pretty skirt and Paul's sweater, instead of a tacky print dress. That was one good thing at least. She took off her coat but couldn't find a nail to hang it on. She started to lay it on a chair.

Dolly quickly took the coat from her. "Here, I'll hang it in the hall closet. Reela had this closet built jist for the purpose of hanging up visitors' coats. She's got ever'-thang. Ain't it somethin'? My gosh, Naomi, where'd you get that ghastly orange sweater?"

What could Dolly mean? This was a turtleneck. Mary Jean wore a turtleneck. Why, she'd even seen Dolly once in a turtleneck. What did a body say when someone said something like that? If it'd been Mom or Grace, she'd have yelled right back. But Dolly Russel . . .

Mary Jean said, "Don't be so smart, Dolly. Reela likes orange too. Lots of things in this room is orange!"

"Look, I didn't mean nothin', but for gosh sakes, Reela knows what colors to wear orange with. And the shade is important. Come on, I'll show you. I was gonna show you Reela's clothes anyway." Dolly led them into the bedroom over to a newly built closet that ran the entire length of the room. She reached into the closet and took out a beautiful soft wool skirt of deep, deep orange. She handed it to Naomi.

Naomi stood there holding up the hanger. She knew at once that Reela was just her size. Then Dolly handed her a blouse that was the lightest orange one could imagine. It was so thin and soft, it had to be pure silk. Naomi lay it against the skirt. The ruffles of the blouse, the softness of the wool—why, she never knew clothes could look like that.

"Wanta try them on?" Dolly asked. Naomi didn't know how her face looked when Dolly said that, but it must have been funny because Dolly started laughing. "Go on, it won't bite you, try it on. You too, Mary Jean. Come on, we'll all do it. Reela will never know. You cain't hurt a dress by tryin' it on."

Dolly wasn't so bad after all. In fact, she was lots of fun to visit with. Naomi had never had so much fun in her entire life as she and Mary Jean and Dolly had trying on Reela's dresses and skirts and shoes and everything. Of course nothing fit Dolly, which made things more fun than ever, and Mary Jean wasn't a whole lot better. But with Naomi . . . well, they were perfect.

Naomi was a tall girl like Reela—no, a tall *woman* like Reela. Never was Naomi more sure that her womanhood was upon her than when she looked at the beautiful image of herself wearing Reela's magnificent clothes. She gazed into the mirror as if it were another world, or a dream— yes, one of her daydreams.

Finally she said, "I'm beautiful. I really am. I had no idea!"

Dolly said, "See what I mean? That is a ghastly sweater, now isn't it? When I get married, I'm going to get me a man who can buy me beautiful clothes like these. What you say, Mary Jean, it'd sure beat us workin' in the dime store, wouldn't it?"

Mary Jean didn't answer. Mary Jean was stripped nude and was slipping on a long blue satin nightgown.

"Hey!" Dolly cried, and ran to get one for herself. She handed Naomi one in cream-colored chiffon with fold after fold of the billowy material just waiting to touch her skin.

Naomi had never undressed completely in front of any girl, not even Grace, except in the bathtub when they were little or when they were changing clothes late at night. In the daytime they undressed in the big closet below the staircase. It didn't seem to bother Dolly or Mary Jean, though, and, after all, they were only girls.

Naomi got into the gown and stood in front of the mirror again. Never in all her life had she seen anything so beautiful. So tall and slender she looked. So old, so . . . Whatever was that? Laughter . . . and whistles, lots of whistles. It was men!

"The window!" shouted Dolly. "Good gosh, we forgot to pull the shade."

Naomi ran as she'd never run before and pulled the shade way down below the bottom of the window. The very nerve of those soldiers to stand down there and spy! The very nerve to yell and whistle like that. She was mad enough to . . . She pulled back the side of the shade enough for her to raise the window a bit. She stuck her face to the cold air and yelled, "Y'ought to be ashamed of yourselves. Everyone of you ought to be ashamed of yourselves!"

Dolly and Mary Jean pulled her away so she didn't hear what the soldiers yelled back, and she didn't care!

Dolly said, "Come on, Naomi, you cain't make a soldier feel ashamed."

"Besides, you're about to freeze us all to death." Mary Jean was already putting her own clothes back on. Naomi started to get back into her own clothes, and so did Dolly.

Dolly said, "I don't know why we're all dressin'. We

ought to be puttin' on nightgowns anyway to go to bed. Go ahead and change. I'm going to make sure the door downstairs is locked."

That was a good idea. Naomi was glad to know the door was locked. Doors on her house had never been locked that she ever knew of. Dad said most people were honest, and Mom said no one ever stole from the poor anyway. Naomi had never even thought to be afraid of a man. Why, her house had always been protected by Dad and her brothers.

Soon they had their own nightclothes on. Mary Jean had brought a nightgown, but Naomi always slept in her slip. Dolly grabbed the bowl of popcorn, and they all three crawled into Reela's bed.

Mary Jean said, "Want me to tell a ghost story? It'll help us get our minds off those awful soldiers. You believe in ghosts?"

Naomi said, "I don't believe in ghosts, but I love ghost stories, so go ahead."

"You better believe in ghosts!" said Dolly. "I read where some scientists are studying this stuff, and they actually proved there are ghosts and that there's a lot of truth in some fortune-telling too. It's called ESP."

Naomi didn't want to have anything proved. "Dolly, it's not true. Dad says it ain't true at all. My teachers at school jist laugh at ghost stories and . . . well, where did you read that?"

"Reela has a book on it. I'll show you."

Dolly came back with a book on the subject, all right, and as much as Naomi hated to have proof, she could not help but reach for it and begin to read. She read aloud until everybody was tired of listening and talking and had decided to go to sleep.

Dolly got up and turned off the electric light, then jumped back into bed to nestle in close to Naomi and Mary Jean.

Three in bed made a tight fit, but tonight Naomi was glad for it. She'd sure hate to be sleeping alone.

Mary Jean said, "All right, now, if any of you want to turn over, jist yell spoon, and then we'll all turn at once. Okay?"

"Okay," Naomi muttered, and then tried to clear her mind so she could fall asleep.

She dreamed she had to take a pill. She needed to take a pill for what ailed her. She found the bottle sitting in the middle of the table. It was a big bottle and chuck full of pills of all sizes and shapes. Which one should she take? Which one should she take? It bothered her something furious until she started shouting "Eeny meeny miny, Moe." Then she grabbed one, and she had started to put it into her mouth when . . . Was that Mary Jean yelling "Spoon"? No, it was someone downstairs knocking on the door and shouting.

Mary Jean and Dolly were awake now too and clutching each other. That voice, Naomi would know that voice anywhere. It was Dad.

"Dolly, y'better let me go unlock the door or Dad will bust it in." Naomi slipped Paul's turtleneck sweater on and jumped into her purple corduroy skirt, hoping Dad would hold off until she got down the stairs. He settled down when she started to unlock the door. It was still nighttime. What was Dad doing . . . The door opened.

"Naomi, find your coat and git your shoes on. You're comin' home!"

"What's the matter, Dad? What's happened?"

"You know what's happened and the whole country knows. I didn't tell you you could stay all night in this soldier town! This—this town of sapsuckers. I want my willow tall an' clean an' . . . I didn't tell you to ask for no job in this soldier town! And you young ladies . . ." Dad

172

looked toward Dolly and Mary Jean at the head of the stairs. "I'll leave y'to your own dads, but remember this, neither of you is to be seen with Naomi agin."

Dad dragged Naomi and pushed her into the front seat of the pickup. "Naomi, y'll never amount to a hill of beans!" He slammed the door. It was cold in the truck.

All the way home Naomi sat on the front seat as far away from Dad as possible and let tears stream as they would. Dad hated crying of any sort, she knew that, but he never made a move to stop her.

When they got home, the lights were all lighted, and everyone was still up. Grace sat behind the heating stove with Lenny. Pete and Paul sat to one side of the heater with their bare feet on the warming bar. Bruce and Benny sat in the doorway next to the stairs picking dried cockleburs out of old Spot's fur. Jay wasn't home, or else he had chosen to stay in bed.

Mom stood in front of the heater with the first words. "I told you, Naomi, the Lord won't have no mercy. I've warned y'a million times. I'll take no blame."

"What's the matter? I ain't done nothin' bad!"

Paul said, "Naomi, it seems y'didn't spend all night wearin' my turtleneck sweater, accordin' to the word that got around to one of Lenny's buddies. And Pete heard the same thang from someone else."

Grace said, "It's goin' to be hard on us all havin' to face people."

Mom yelled, "Facin' people ain't the half of it. Puttin' on a show before soldiers! There ain't a decent man in this country who'll marry a woman who's showed her nakedness to a whole town full of soldiers!"

Naomi stood there looking at them. All of them, her whole family, believing the worst, not one of them asking her to explain.

If she told them all about it, if she told them from beginning to end, then maybe they'd . . . She looked at their faces, some more bitter than others, but none smiling, none saying, "Naomi, straighten this out for us." For the first time Naomi understood why Sarah had not explained things to Preacher Haller for all those years.

She didn't know what she would do. She wasn't old enough to leave home, and she felt sure Dad wouldn't ask her to do that. Mom was standing there right this minute thinking that Naomi was to be a burden forever like Aunt Wilma, and Naomi knew that, but she'd have to stay for a while longer and be a burden. Naomi hung her head out of weariness from the problem.

Mom was crying now. She'd never seen Mom cry. "Mom, I never knowed that them soldiers was . . ."

"Don't make it worse with excuses. Knowed or not knowed, they was lustin' after you. They was there, and they saw your nakedness." The soldiers were whistling and laughing. Was laughing the same as lusting? Mom's voice grew louder. "Lord help us, Naomi, you've lost ever' chance y'ever had. There ain't no second chances." Great sobs burst from Mom now, and she talked through the violence of her weeping. "Ruth was my favorite story in the Bible. Ruth said to Naomi, the Bible Naomi, 'My God is your God. Where you go I go.' I named you before y'was born, Naomi. I always liked that name 'Naomi.' I always wished it was my own name and that I could have me a daughter that'd want to follow me and do the right thing and not fight against me and my ways. I've prayed for you, Naomi. Lord knows I prayed." Mom's body shook uncontrollably.

Finally, everyone went to bed. Naomi took off Paul's turtleneck sweater and laid it on the stairs. Then she crawled into the single bed in the room she shared with the twins. She hadn't meant to hurt Mom so. What was it all about?

Naomi lay on her bed thinking. Mom had never told her before the whole story of why she had picked the name Naomi. She had never seen Mom cry before. She had seen her shout and scream and hit, but never cry. The crying was the worst.

Naomi wasn't bad just because Mom thought she was bad. Maybe it was bad to show your nakedness before an audience, but it hadn't been her plan to do that. She would never do it again. It was easy to repent of an accidental sin, because once you found it out, you knew right off it wouldn't happen again. God knew that. God wouldn't be worrying and crying about it. What would get God worried would be if she did something wrong and didn't want to stop doing it. But she could never explain that to Mom. She and Mom didn't think alike. It would be hard for her to follow Mom like Ruth.

Naomi lay there and thought of the story of Ruth. Just last week she had read it. She liked to see her own name in the Bible; it gave her a warm feeling somehow. That Naomi in the Bible was a great woman all right. First she offered Ruth the right to be herself and go wherever she wanted to go. Now wouldn't it be nice if Mom and Dad and everybody would do the very same thing?

Mom's sobs and voice were growing loud in the other room. "Oh, how I prayed this would never happen, but somethin' inside me knowed that it would."

Instead of Mom's sobs touching Naomi this time, they raised an anger within her, a terrible fierce anger that seemed to give her a mighty strength. Yes, Mom had known something bad would happen, and Grace had known. People all over had, by their knowing, invited her to follow them in "knowing" the worst would happen to Naomi Bradley. And she had watched with the others waiting for the evil and illness to happen, waiting for her own destruction before God. Well, she would not have anyone telling her who she was, or what she'd do, or how soon she ought to marry, or how she'd turn out, or even if she'd die or not. She was tired of listening to the voices of others. She had a voice of her own. A feeling of her own! Didn't she? Well, didn't she?

ELEVEN

The snow made the world quiet, entirely too quiet. There was no peace in the quietness now. It was as if God had joined right in with the rest of the family in not wanting to talk to her anymore. That was just fine. Naomi didn't need to talk to anyone. She could manage for herself. She wasn't listening to anyone's talk anymore.

Even when Pete and Paul returned after an afternoon on the sled, with Queenie hooked up alongside Jill to pull it, and with Abe along as an extra passenger, Naomi still thought she wouldn't talk to anyone. Abe finally got her to one side and said, "Hey, Naomi, why the long face?"

"Ain't y'heard? Everybody in the whole country's heard."

"Look, the way I'm able to piece the story together, it seems a bunch of soldiers got a free show and the family is makin' you pay a big price for it. I bet you don't undress agin without checkin' to see if the shade's pulled." Abe was laughing.

"It ain't funny, Abe. You don't see Mom or Dad laughin'. I don't wont people laughin' about it anyway. Ever'body's thinkin' the worst, or maybe some's like you, and are laughin' at me. When I was little, I wanted ever'body in the

177

whole world to like me, and now I don't care if nobody does. And nobody does. I'm forgittin' all about ever'body and about ever'thang that's ever happened to me." Naomi realized she was getting dramatic, but she could do that with Abe.

"That cain't work, Naomi. A body don't forgit their past. Y'either accept it till it don't bother y' no more, or you're going to have it still hangin' on. Now if you'd really forgotten it, y'wouldn't be havin' such a long face. You'd be best to look on that window business as an experience and nothin' more."

"At first I did, Abe, but Mom and Dad nor anyone else did. I cain't feel that way about it anymore. How can I when Mom's yellin' and . . ."

But she knew. She had known it when she got so mad. If she did her own thinking, listened to her own voice, then she could call it an experience. It hadn't been bad just because other people said it was. She looked at Abe again and started laughing.

Abe said, "You keep them eyes open and y'll see a lot of folks who still care for you." Then he slapped her on the arm and yelled, "I'll race y' to the sled."

Mom yelled, "Naomi, you stay in this house. You can core these apples now that your barn chores are done."

Mom got up, and Naomi took her place in the chair next to Grace. She started coring and cutting while Grace peeled.

"Hey, Grace, you're skippin' places. Wont to do this'n over?"

"No. Jist cut it out and go on. It's for applesauce. No one will ever know the difference." Grace looked tired and pale. Was she still upset about what happened?

Grace got up suddenly and ran out to vomit in the snow. So that was it. Grace was pregnant. Well now, wonder how it'd feel being an aunt?

Naomi finished the rest of the apples herself and took them to the stove, where Mom was busy cooking the first of them. Mom took them without a word and turned back to the stove. There was no use staying here and standing close to hate and hurt. A sweet cinnamon smell filled the kitchen, and it seemed all wrong, considering.

Naomi went to the front room to see if the twins had gotten out of their wet clothes yet. They were both in their long underwear sitting next to Dad watching him breathe as he lay back in the rocker fast asleep. His book had dropped, and his reading glasses had fallen to one side.

Bruce said, "Listen, Naomi, listen."

Dad's breath would go slow and easy for a while, then with a jerk he'd inhale deeply. Benny said, "That sounds scary, don't it? Sounds like he's goin' to die, don't it?"

"Benny, for gosh sakes, cut out that kind of talk. Both of you, go git your pants on." Naomi scolded so sharply that Dad woke up. He looked at her at first the way he would at anyone, being woken up the way he was. Then he got a remembering look on his face and closed his eyes, pretending to go back to sleep.

Naomi didn't ask permission, but she got her coat on and went back outside. She guessed she'd just take a walk over to see Sarah Haller.

The snow was pretty. God had made everybody's place look neat and clean and beautiful. It was the only time when Sarah's house looked no better than those of her neighbors. Naomi noticed that Sarah's oil heater didn't raise the same kind of smoke out of a chimney that a good wood fire did.

She wondered what Sarah was doing. There were no tracks outside as yet this morning. She knocked on the door.

"Naomi! Well, come in. Is everything all right?" Naomi stepped inside, but Sarah stood at the door for a moment.

Naomi said, "I guess I'm all right. I guess you have always to ask a question like that, don't you? Jay said that you and Preacher Haller had to keep the whole country's body and soul together. Don't y'ever git tired of seein' no one but ailin' people?"

"Cold out, isn't it? Pretty, though, don't you think? We don't need flowers in the winter, do we?" Sarah seemed reluctant to close the door, but she finally did. "What did you say? Oh, do I get tired of . . . I see other people besides the ailing. I see you, Naomi."

Naomi hung her head. She waited for Sarah to start talking about her being naked in front of the soldiers.

"There's not anything wrong with you, is there, Naomi?"

"Ain't y'heard about what happened in Malden?"

"No, do you want to tell me?"

Not everyone knew, anyway. It stood to reason folks wouldn't gossip much to Sarah, but surely someone had told Preacher Haller by now. "Where's Preacher Haller?"

"Oh, he's gone, didn't you know? He's gone to a seminary conference in Memphis for six weeks. He's always wanted to go to school but never had the chance. I told him there was no better time to be gone than in the winter. A lot of people don't attend church then, anyway. So he went. Did you need to talk to him, Naomi?"

"No, I don't have to talk to him, jist wondered why he wasn't here. I sort of wanted to talk to you. I guess I'll have to start by tellin' you about what happened, or else you won't know what I'm talkin' about later."

Naomi told Sarah all that happened at Malden and at home and how she was going to decide for herself who she was and whether she was good or bad.

Sarah smiled. "I understand. I understand completely, Naomi."

"No, y'don't understand completely, 'cause you're not me. I ain't exactly like you, nor nobody else, as far as that

180

goes. But I'm glad y'ain't mad at me and I thank you for that. I didn't reckon y'd be mad, but like I say, nothin's certain."

"Nothing, Naomi?" Sarah was wanting her to talk more, but she wasn't sure what it was that she'd wanted to talk about. Sarah didn't rush her.

At last Naomi felt as if she would explode if the question didn't come and it came. "I ain't listenin' to nobody, I ain't followin' nobody, but I don't know what I am doin'. What am I goin' to do, Sarah Haller?"

"Sit down here at the table beside me, Naomi. Let me make you some hot chocolate." Sarah got up and made the chocolate in no time, on the electric hot plate. Naomi took it, poured some over a slice of light bread, and watched as it slowly seeped its color into the whiteness of the bread. "If only I knew how to start thinkin', how to start plannin'. I don't mean dreamin'. I wont these to be real plans. I wont them to work."

"All right, what's your goal?"

"My what? Oh, I don't know. I wont to do what I'm good at." Naomi remembered when she'd thought that she was good at preaching. Then there was the time when she'd hoped to be good at cooking or doing important field work like planting and hay baling, and she had never made it. "I guess I ain't good at nothin' except arithmetic."

"What do you mean? You were certainly good in helping me with Mrs. Jackson and Faith and Faith's children. You're good with little children, Naomi. Why, I'm sure there are *many* things you can do. You still have a lot of schooling ahead of you. I said before I thought you'd make a good nurse, and I still think it. If you want to go in that direction, let me know. Too bad you're not old enough right now. Now that I'm pregnant, I find that—"

"You too? Grace is goin' to have a baby, too. My gosh, it seems that jist ever'body is goin' to have a baby. My gosh,

Sarah Haller, I didn't know that you was goin' to have a baby!"

Sarah looked very pleased. "See what I mean, Naomi? You'd be splendid working in obstetrics. How could any expectant mother not respond to your enthusiasm?"

"And you could teach me how to help 'em so they wouldn't be so scared, and then they'd have it easier havin' their baby, and I could bathe the baby like you did Faith's and —" Suddenly Naomi realized that she was daydreaming again. She felt ashamed to have dreamed out loud in front of Sarah.

It didn't seem to bother Sarah at all. "Of course I will. Of course you could. There's no reason why you can't. All right, there's your goal! Begin your planning. There are scholarships, you know. I'll help you when you get to that point."

The planning set in her head at once. She'd help people like Mrs. Jackson. Nobody would have to be scared to death of dying if she, Naomi Bradley, was there. She'd be the best nurse in all the world. Daydreaming was sort of like giving yourself a little gift, and it was nothing to be ashamed of if it was tacked on to some real plans or, like Sarah Haller put it, a real goal. Naomi felt so good she finished her chocolate-soaked bread and got up to go back and face her family at home. She could face anyone now!

As she trudged home in the deep snow, she let her dreams go higher and higher until she got to thinking that there was no use wasting all this time. Sarah needed her help right now. She changed her path and started wading the snow in toward Malden to see Dr. Foster.

He was in his office, and she took no time to dawdle. She asked him, straight out, if she couldn't be of some help to him and Sarah after school and on Saturdays.

"Well now, if you ain't the little banty—I guess I cain't say rooster, can I? Anyway, I think we can use you. That doctor in Dexter got drafted, and that just makes more work than one man can handle. I said last week that it's a shame Sarah wasn't a man because we could sure use another doctor. I say right now I'm wishing she was a man so she'd not be pregnant and me having to look forward to the day when her work hours will slack."

On her way home through the snow, Naomi felt free and had not one qualm as she let her dreams fly again. So they needed another doctor, did they? And Dr. Foster wasn't the youngest man in the world either. Someday they'd really be in bad need of a doctor around here. As long as she was going to go to school and study up on medicine and stuff, she'd just as well be a doctor so she could find out what it took to stop cancer. Then people like Mrs. Jackson wouldn't have to die. She'd be the best woman doctor a body ever heard of. Naomi stopped her daydream to face facts. She'd best keep this dream a secret for a while.

When she first started work for Dr. Foster, she wondered if people would stay away because of what had happened at Malden. Mom and Dad had worried about it, when she told them she had the job, but neither of them tried to stop her from helping Dr. Foster. Everybody liked him. Dad said it might even help people to forget what happened if they saw that Dr. Foster was willing to let her be his help. Naomi wasn't sure whether it was that reason or the reason that people can forget a lot of things if they are in need of help. Anyway, people came to the office, and Naomi worked the best she could. She answered the phone and helped track down Dr. Foster when he was out on calls, and she tried to make it easier for people to wait in the office until he returned.

Around school there was still some talk about what had happened at the window in Malden, and lots of boys laughed and gave Naomi a hard time of it. Certainly Troy Donly, her friendly rival in math classes, tried to be nice. Surely he was one of the friends that Abe told her she'd see if she kept her eyes open and looked for them. But she didn't want to talk to Troy. She wasn't much in the mood to talk to any boy for a while.

One day Troy showed up at Dr. Foster's office when she was working. No one was in the office, and Dr. Foster was gone, so Troy sat in a chair and tried to talk. He didn't have any trouble about talking when it came to discussing how to work an arithmetic problem, but now he sat silent in the waiting-room chair. Naomi thought he'd never say what he'd come to say.

Finally, Troy stood up and said, "Naomi, I never did laugh. I know y'musta felt awful. I sure would've, if the situation had been turned around."

For a moment Naomi tried to imagine Troy trying on a new suit in front of an upstairs window with a whole streetful of girls standing below, laughing and whistling and calling. She gave up. "Y'don't know how I felt."

"Maybe not, but I know y'didn't do nothin' bad. I know y'd never do nothin' bad on purpose." That was a lot for Troy to say, and he'd gotten worked up doing it. It was nice of him to say it. Naomi wondered what he was going to do now that he had. What could she say back to him?

Troy made no motion to leave but continued to sit and watch. The door opened again. Mrs. Medlain and her oldest boy Freddie came in. Freddie was crying. Mrs. Medlain said, "Freddie's been poisoned! We had fish for dinner, and all was goin' nice till Freddie got up and went to the milk crock, unbeknown to me, and drunk some milk. We've told him a hundred times that eatin' fish and milk in the same meal would poison a body, but he don't listen to a word we say."

"He ain't poisoned, Mrs. Medlain. Dr. Foster says there

ain't no truth to that tale. But you wait and tell him when he gits in if you wont."

The furrows of worry and concern left Mrs. Medlain's eyes, but she waited. So did Troy. Troy didn't say any more, he just waited and watched until Dr. Foster got in. Then he left.

Dr. Foster said, "What'd that young man want?"

"I don't know. He never said."

Dr. Foster shrugged and went on with his work. Naomi did know what Troy had wanted to say, sort of. Someday, when she was much older . . . anyway, it was reassuring to know there would be men in the world like Troy. Like Abe said, if she kept her eyes open, she'd find a lot of people to her liking who also liked her.

She gave no more thought to Troy until a few days later when Grace mentioned him. Mom was saying, "Naomi, don't get so caught up in that job of yourn that y'forgit that the Lord'll expect you to find yourself a man and make a home of your own one of these days."

Grace said, "I hear there's a boy been hangin' out around Dr. Foster's office that's got his eye on her."

Now who told Grace about Troy? *He* sure wouldn't have mentioned it. Did Mrs. Medlain? Could be. Grace should keep her nose out of other people's affairs. "Grace, you know Troy ain't thinkin' about marryin' me or anybody else right now. And I doubt he'd want to wait around eight years to git me."

"What do you mean, eight years?" Mom shouted. "No daughter of mine is hangin' around home for eight years. That's the number of years I put up with Wilma, but if you thank for one minute that gives you the right to do the same, you got another thank comin'!"

Naomi hadn't meant to say that about eight years. She wasn't sure just how long it'd be. She'd just said a number. She'd been so aggravated with Grace it just slipped out.

But Mom was going to have to know sooner or later. "I ain't hangin' around home that long, Mom. I'm going away to school. It takes a long time to be a doctor."

"Careful now, Naomi. Y'got no right to talk hifalutin to your own mother. The Lord'll hear y'talkin' boastful! Don't kindle His wrath."

Mom was thinking more than she was saying, and Naomi knew it. Mom's face looked scared, concerned. Mom was thinking about Naomi's fourteenth birthday being less than two weeks away. She knew that in spite of outward talk, Mom and Grace both were mindful of the fact. Nobody cared to discuss the matter right out loud, and that was fine with Naomi. She didn't want to think of it. She wanted to get caught up in her work.

However, a thing like your meeting with death can only be pushed out of the way for so long, and then something will come to remind you again. At the supper table, Pete said, "There was a priest come into Malden today. I saw him. He wears long robes like some old lady's dress and walks with his back straight as a stick. He's goin' to set up church in one of the Quonset huts for the Catholic soldiers."

Mom stopped eating, pushed back her chair, and started to fan her face with her apron tail. "God help us all! I've prayed for three long years agin it, but that woman's got the power. Ever' last thang she's said has come true. Ever' last thang! Poor Naomi. Poor, poor Naomi!"

Dad had been sipping his coffee from a saucer. At Mom's words he slammed it down on the table, splashing it all over the beans. "Cut it out! I won't hear it. It's a bunch of hogwash and ain't no cause for us to worry!"

Everyone was worrying, Naomi could tell. Well, she wouldn't let them. It had been too hard to get her own self thinking in the right direction to chance backsliding. "I ain't dyin'."

"What makes y'so sure?" Grace asked too fast, showing

at once where her feelings lay and what she believed.

"I ain't, 'cause I ain't. Jist like I ain't goin' to be a lot of thangs that people says I am. I jist ain't, that's all." Naomi rose from the table and turned away from them.

"Okay, *I* believe you." Paul gulped down the last of his milk and started to leave the table. "You sure as hell have me convinced, Naomi."

"I believe you," said Benny. And "I believe you," echoed Bruce.

Nobody else said anything after all that, but Naomi felt better.

In the coming days Mom showed what she believed. She made Naomi a beautiful dress of soft cream cotton and sewed two rows of gold rickrack around the edge.

Mom meant well—Naomi knew that—but she had no intention of being an angel again. She wasn't going to fly off to heaven in a pretty dress. She thought about it for hours at night, and wished she had Preacher Haller to talk to. But he wasn't back yet, so she had no out but to do her own thinking again. Now, if she were God, what would she do? For one thing, she'd not ever make someone suffer for no reason.

The next night was her last supper before her birthday. She decided to put minds at rest again. She said, "God don't want people to die young. If it happens, it ain't His doin', but an accident. And if you keep the faith, He won't even let that happen, He'll protect you. Now which would you rather have me do, keep the faith in God or in Mrs. Jeno?"

Paul got up from the table and said, "We seen more proof from Mrs. Jeno than God!"

"Lord help us all! That's blasphemy!" Mom started fanning herself.

Paul tripped on the table leg, and Naomi started hitting him with both fists.

"Naomi, you missed your callin'; y'ought to been a preacher."

"Y'won't have to listen to me no more! I won't cast my pearls before swine!"

Mom said, "Lord, Lord, Lord! Dad, do something. Stop them. Paul, such talk, and tomorrer bein' Naomi's birthday! You'll call disaster down on us. The Lord will hear you."

Everyone got real quiet. Grace got up and said, "I'll do the dishes tonight, Naomi. No one's messed up enough dishes for me to even dirty the bottom of a dishpan."

Dad said, "Git in bed, all of you. We've got a day's work ahead of us tomorrer. I wont to clean out the horse stalls. First thang y'know it'll be thawin' and time to start in the fields agin." Everyone seemed glad to obey Dad. Naomi knew Dad's real reason and guessed bed was about the safest place to be all right.

It got dark early in the winter, but it was cold and bright with the stars out and snow still on the ground. The twins crawled into their double bed, and Naomi got into her single one nearby. She lay there and tried not to think.

What was that last sermon Preacher Haller gave before taking off on that trip? Let's see, he had said, "God don't comfort us to make us comfortable but to make us comforters." He'd explained it too, but she couldn't for the life of her remember that part. Tomorrow she'd have to start remembering things. She did remember how scared she had been when she had first taken up the idea to preach. She thought she'd probably do better as a doctor.

Everything had gone just fine for her working for Dr. Foster. That was the way it had been in her life. Sometimes she'd felt strong and fine, sometimes scared and weak. How strong she'd felt that time she'd decided she could do her own thinking, plan her own life. She had been mad then, but she'd sure felt nice and strong. Now that was a funny thing: She hardly ever felt mad and scared and weak at the same time. Maybe never. Maybe if she got real mad tonight, maybe she'd not be scared at all. Now she knew why she had enjoyed hitting Paul tonight. How did he know she needed to be mad? Or did he? Poor Mom, she was so scared. . . .

Suddenly Naomi sat up in bed.

"What's the matter, Naomi, you sick?"

"No, Bruce, you go back to sleep. I jist thought of somethin' I never thought of before."

Mom had always been so mean, and she was always striking Naomi. But she was scared too! Mom had always been scared: scared she'd not have a daughter to be proud of; scared that Grace might not be pretty enough to get a man; scared that there might not be enough food for the whole winter; scared she'd have to stand next to Aunt Wilma all her life; and scared that the Lord might strike Naomi dead for being different. Mom, that's not like God at all. Something's all mixed up here. God loves people, doesn't He? It's the devil that doesn't love people. It's fear that makes people suffer and suffer and suffer. The devil is fear. Naomi shot up in bed again.

"What's a matter, Naomi, you dyin'?" Benny cried.

"No, no, Benny, I ain't dyin'. I jist had another thought, sort of a silly-crazy thought, but a new thought all the same."

"Don't have no more new thoughts, okay?"

"I won't, Benny, I promise."

But no sooner had she said it than she jumped up again. "Benny! Bruce! Come here. I want to tell you somethin'." The boys came and tried to squeeze into bed with her. "Did you know that settin' a goal is almost the same as a fortune-teller sayin' somethin'."

"What's a goal?"

"Well, it's this thing that you plan all by yourself. You decide jist what you want to have happen, and it will happen. Like I want to be a doctor, and already here I am workin' for Dr. Foster, makin' my own livin', and gittin' to watch him and learn the art of doctorin'."

"Can I do it? What makes it work?" The boys weren't acting scared anymore.

What did make it work? Naomi didn't know. Why, she didn't even know she wanted to be a doctor until the idea just came up somehow. Then she knew it was the kind of idea she wanted to hang on to.

Why, she'd been hanging on to Mrs. Jeno's words for three years! My gosh, that could be a dangerous thing! She couldn't let another person set her goal. That was her job. Mrs. Jeno had no right to do it, fortune-teller or no. Then Naomi remembered that she had gone and asked Mrs. Jeno. She'd had no business going there in the first place! But she'd only been eleven then, just three years older than Benny and Bruce. She decided to forgive herself on the grounds that she had been too young to know any better.

"You boys git back in your own bed. You're crowdin' me. I'll explain what makes it work another time. Now git to sleep."

Everything was quiet again after the boys got back into their bed and under the pile of quilts. Naomi felt tired— very comfortable and tired. Too bad there wasn't some way she could explain all this to Mom. Poor Mom. What a waste of thinking not to be able to comfort Mom, but it would be a waste of words even to try.

"Naomi, I'm too sleepy to go to sleep." Bruce was sounding scared again.

Naomi got up and walked across the cold floor toward the twins' bed. She stopped to look out the window. An uncertain breeze was whipping this way and that, slapping the willows and swaying the smaller branches of the oak. She'd sleep with the twins. They needed someone to sleep with them.

TWELVE

"Hello. No . . . Naomi is dead."

There was complete silence on the telephone for a moment. Then Abe said, "All right, Naomi, I know your voice. Happy birthday!"

"Thanks, Abe. I'm mighty glad to hear you say that."

"You wouldn't mind if me and Mabel come over for a little while today, would you? We got somethin' to tell you."

"Don't tell me Mabel is pregnant. No wonder Dr. Foster needs a helper! Well, is she?"

"Mabel wonts to tell it herself. Now don't blab it around. Say, what do you mean teasin' me about being dead? Death ain't nothin' to tease about."

"I wasn't teasin'. Naomi *is* dead. The old scaredy-cat Naomi is dead. She died last night."

"Hold all that silly talk. We'll be over for a visit."

By the time Mabel and Abe arrived, Mom was cooking a big Sunday dinner, and Grace was baking a plain birthday cake, two yellow layers with a little jelly spread between them. Naomi was . . . well, Naomi was peeling potatoes, in beautiful, long, thin spirals, paper-thin peels. Out of habit she threw the spiral over her shoulder, but did not look to see the initial. It might not agree with the initial of the man that she herself would pick someday.

Abe said, "My, that's a right pretty dress you're wearin', Naomi. I can't for the life of me figure who you take after. You peel that potater like Mom, dress as pretty as my Mabel or Aunt Wilma, but from all I hear, you run that doctor's office good as Dr. Foster hisself. What's this Grace was sayin' about you havin' a feller? When you gettin' married, Naomi?"

Naomi didn't get mad at Abe for asking the question. It was a common-enough one to ask a girl just turned fourteen. She looked at Abe, hoping he'd see that she loved him and wasn't acting smart when she answered, "When I please, and to who I please. But first, I'm studyin' to be a doctor so's I can help God add lots of years to lots a people's lives."